# GOD HAD NOT ABANDONED HER...

When Annalisa boarded the plane taking her to America, her future seemed as bleak as her past. She had known so many journeys already, so many departures and arrivals, during her years in war-torn Europe—yet none had ever really changed her life.

*Annalisa did not realize it, but this was to be a new kind of journey for her—a journey not only of the body but of the soul. For though Annalisa had almost abandoned God amid the heart-wrenching events of her life, God had not abandoned her—and the doors of His mercy and grace were about to swing open to receive her at last. . . .*

## SIGNET and MENTOR Books You'll Want to Read

# *Annalisa*

## by Christine Hunter

A SIGNET BOOK

NEW AMERICAN LIBRARY

TIMES MIRROR

# Preface

I FIRST MET "Annalisa" when I was speaking at a women's meeting in California. She attracted me, and when I learned a little of her story, the idea gripped me of putting her in a novel.

Her name is not "Annalisa"; neither do the other characters have their real names. The main items in the story are true, but many details have been filled in from imagination.

I have read the story to "Annalisa." She laughed a little, and wept a lot.

"It is so like yet so unlike my life story," was her comment. "How it brings it all back, and how painful are many of those memories."

Her desire, like mine, is to show the long-suffering and gracious working of a God who never let go.

# 1

————◆————

OFTEN I HAVE WONDERED why life appears to flow along like a placid stream for some people, and for others, it is a series of dangerous rapids and raging torrents.

Looking back over more than seventy years, it is hard for me to remember a time when I could feel relaxed and perfectly happy. Always there has been turmoil and anxiety, even in the only short spell of happiness I enjoyed.

My parents' home was in Switzerland, but my father was killed when I was only ten years old, so my mother had a hard struggle to bring me up on her own.

When I was sixteen, she died of pneumonia, and I went to live with her cousin, who was crippled with polio. She was appointed my legal guardian, and I called her "Aunt" and her husband "Uncle." My "aunt" had no children of her own, but my "uncle" had a son by a previous marriage.

There had been a small amount of money left for me besides my mother's jewelry, and I continued to go to college, but I had a great deal of work to do in the house in the evenings and during the short vacations.

I began to realize very soon that life was going to be difficult for me. As an old woman now, I can look back and realize that I had the kind of beauty which causes a girl heartache and disillusionment. I was very tall and slim; I had vivid blue eyes, long golden hair which I wore in thick braids wound around my head, and a complexion which many people raved about.

If I had had parents to protect me, I am sure life would have been easier, but I was so alone. My aunt was often ill and could not leave her bed or wheelchair without help, so she saw little of what actually went on in the house. As she was my guardian, I never thought of appealing to anyone else for help.

At first, my uncle pretended he wanted me to marry his son—my aunt's stepson, a weak, stupid boy whom I despised; then he himself started pestering me with attentions. He would wait until no one else was present, then try to make passes at me, until I was terrified of being alone with him.

One night, when I was eighteen, he came to my room, and only by fighting like a tiger did I manage to get away from him, and lock myself in a small bathroom.

The next day, I told my aunt what had happened, and I will never forget the sad, hopeless expression on her face. "You are not the only one," she said with no emotion in her voice. "But you must get away. I'll help you if I can. I have a little money of my own, and after you have gone, I'll try to get whatever there is left from your mother's money, and send it to you. Take her jewelry with you. Some of the pieces have been handed down in the family, and although they may be old-fashioned, they are valuable. Someday if you are in desperate need, you may be obliged to sell them. But where can you go to be safe?"

"I will go to Marie DuBois in Geneva. We were friends at school, and once I helped her escape when the building caught on fire. She has often written, asking me to stay with her family. They will help me to get work, I am sure."

Hastily, I gathered my belongings together, sent a telegram to Marie, and unknown to my uncle, I set off for Geneva.

Marie's whole family was waiting for me, and showed me tremendous kindness, insisting that I must look upon their house as my home from now on.

Besides Marie and her parents, there were two brothers and a divorced sister living at home, and at first everything was very enjoyable.

I loved Geneva. Everywhere I looked, there was a vista of majestic beauty which made me catch my breath in delight.

How beautiful Lake Geneva was, with its white-winged sailing boats and steamers, against the background of dark green trees and majestic Mont Blanc, always capped with snow, towering into the blue sky in France, on the southern border of the lake.

Marie's sister, Luci, ran a bookshop down by the lakeside; she was in need of another assistant, and would be glad if I would work for her. I accepted with delight. What could be more enjoyable than to work among the books I loved, and to be able to look out continually on such a feast of beauty? Also, hundreds of foreign tourists visited Geneva every year; so I would meet many interesting people.

I soon began to realize that again I was to have no peace. Marie's oldest brother, Edo, began to pester me; and if he saw me talking to any man in the shop, he was wild with jealousy. It was his responsibility at night to close up the shop and to accompany me home, and how I hated those evening walks.

At last, I made up my mind that I would have to move to another place; but I had no idea where I could go, certainly not back to my guardian.

One day, by telephone I was asked to take some books to a customer's house. When I got there an elderly gentleman I had noticed in the shop several times opened the door.

"Please come in and rest, until I decide if these are the books I require," he said very politely, inviting me into a lounge and offering me a chair. He pretended to examine the books, then said, "Excuse me a moment." He returned with a tray, upon which there were glasses and a decanter.

"Allow me to offer you some wine," he said gallantly, but by this time all I wanted was to get out of the house.

"No, thank you, I must hurry back," I said, standing up and edging toward the door.

"I feel it my duty to tell you that a nice, innocent girl of such beauty should not live with the type of people you are with now," he began, and I stared in surprise. "I know a great deal about them that is not to their credit. I realize that you are of a quite different class—your manners and speech show it. I believe you have no parents to protect you, so please let me help you. Come here and live with me, and you will have money, clothes, and everything you desire."

My heart was beating furiously, for now I realized what he was suggesting; but trying to be as calm as possible, I said, "Thank you for your thoughtfulness, but I must think it over."

"Very well, but remember this is between you and me. If you confide in the family with whom you live, they will never let you go. Take this little gift to show you that I mean what I say," and offering me a small jewel box, he snapped open the lid, and held out a beautiful bracelet.

I shook my head. "I could not accept such a gift," I said firmly. "You will have your answer very soon," and pulling open the front door, I almost ran down the steps.

I rushed to the lakeside; and forgetting all about the shop, I threw myself down on the grass in the shelter of some trees, my body shaking with fright.

Why was I never allowed to live in peace? Why did every man I met have only one thought in mind? Were there no decent people whom I could trust? Where could I go? I certainly would never allow Marie's brother or this horrible old man to ruin my life.

Then I remembered that earlier in the day a customer had inquired if we knew of anyone who could act as his secretary and copy out a book he was writing. Marie's sister had told me that this dark-eyed, black-haired stranger was an Arab scholar who had come to Switzerland because of his health, together with his stepmother, who was a titled English lady, or as we would say, a baroness.

I was proud of my own handwriting; and that night I wrote a letter, which I handed to him the next day. He seemed surprised, then asked why I wanted to leave the shop. I replied that I felt I would like a change, and that if my handwriting was good enough for him, I would like to copy out the work he required.

He said, "I will think it over and let you know tomorrow." I waited in a fever of impatience until he appeared the next day.

"I have decided that you will be useful as my secretary," he said when there was no one else within earshot. "But where will you live?"

"I must get away from the place where I am at once," I said, and he must have realized that I was desperate.

"Come to this address tomorrow, and we will discuss the possibilities," he said, handing me a card.

The next day, inventing some sort of excuse, I slipped out, and made for the address he had given me.

An elderly woman opened the door, and eyed me up and down. "Monsieur Poitier is expecting you," she said coldly, and turning back into the hall, knocked on a door.

"A young woman to see you, sir," she said, and gave the door a slam behind her.

"Frau Kramper does not approve of my having a secretary to live in the house," he said. "Up until now, I have only employed one from time to time by the day."

"I'm not really a secretary," I replied, wanting to be perfectly honest.

"I realize that, but I think you will be able to meet my requirements. Of course, you realize, there will be long hours of weary copying to be done. I cannot pay a big wage, but you will have your room and your food free."

"Can I come at once?" I asked desperately.

"Why are you so anxious to leave your present employment?"

I felt my face flushing, as I said, with an effort to meet his eyes, "Because circumstances have become too much for me. My employer's brother will not leave me alone, and I detest him. There are others also."

He made no reply for a few moments, then turned and stared out of the window, while I waited, wondering if he despised me.

Without looking around, he asked, "You would not be afraid to live here?"

"I think I could trust you," I said, and was amazed at my daring.

"Thank you," he replied simply. "Frau Kramper sleeps here, so you will not be alone, and my stepmother will return shortly. This is her house, but she has gone to England to arrange matters concerning her father's estate; he died recently. I suppose you must give notice to your present employer."

"I only agreed to help until I found other employment."

"Then you can come immediately?"

"I will come tomorrow," I said, determined to get away as soon as possible.

That evening, I packed in secret once more, wrote a note to say that I felt I must leave, but did not reveal where I was going. Then, the next morning, before anyone was awake, I slipped out, carrying my suitcases, and made my way to a taxi stand. It was far too early to present myself at Monsieur Poitier's house, so I went as near to it as I dared; then I waited in a bus shelter until people began to hurry to work.

When I eventually dragged my cases to the door of my new employer, and very hesitantly rang the bell, I dreaded most of all what Frau Kramper would say.

Actually she said practically nothing, but the look on her broad stolid face, with its hard blue eyes, said more than enough.

She made no offer to help me carry my possessions, but silently led the way upstairs. At the end of a short passage, she threw open a door, announcing, "The linen is there; I have no time to make your bed." Then turning, she disappeared.

The room was clean and comfortable enough, but I

wished I could have been welcomed in a kinder manner. However, by now I was used to being treated like this. In a hazy sort of way, young as I was, I realized that my looks were to blame. Women like Frau Kramper thought I could be up to no good. They believed that men wanted me for one thing only, and that I was probably far too free with my favors. I realized it was up to me to alter her opinion.

When I had put my possessions in the drawers and closet, and put out the picture of my beloved mother, I went quietly downstairs.

I was still standing in the hall, when Monsieur Poitier came out of his study.

He jerked in surprise as he caught sight of me. "I did not know you had arrived," he said. "Did Frau Kramper show you to your room?"

"Thank you, yes," I said shyly. "Now I am ready to work."

"Very well, we will begin."

Leading the way into the study, he indicated a table on which were spread a pile of written papers and a pile of unused sheets.

"I am afraid you may have trouble deciphering my handwriting," he said wryly. "I scribble too fast, and I make many alterations. Ask me concerning anything you do not understand."

As I settled myself in a chair, he said, "I must go out this morning." Then he turned back, remarking, "Do not let Frau Kramper upset you. She is not bad at heart, only suspicious."

"Thank you," I replied, and bent to look at the pages before me, my eyes blurred with tears at the kind note in his voice.

Here, I was sure, I had at last found a man who was clean and decent, and did not regard me as a plaything, designed only for his pleasure.

At first I found the rather crabbed writing difficult to undertand, but gradually it became easier. I destroyed the first sheet I had written, because I made several mistakes; then I began to settle down, and by the time

Monsieur Poitier returned, I had several pages ready for his inspection.

He scanned them for several minutes while my heart hammered rapidly, waiting for his approval. At length, he said, "This is better than I had hoped. Now you must stop for lunch. Frau Kramper has suggested that you have a tray in your room, but I would like you to eat with me."

"Thank you, but I would rather have it in my room," I said quietly, knowing that Frau Kramper would object to such familiarity.

"Very well," he replied, and turned to his desk.

I went to my room, washed, tidied my hair, and was standing staring out of the window across the lake and to the far off mountains, when Frau Kramper entered and placed a tray on a small table.

I turned, and summoning up my courage said, "Frau Kramper, this will make a lot of extra work for you."

"That is what I am paid for," she snapped.

"Couldn't I eat with you in your room?" I suggested humbly.

She stared at me, then said, "I eat in the kitchen. You would not consider that good enough."

"Certainly I would. I'm not used to the ways of rich houses, and you could help and advise me, and save me from mistakes."

"Why do your parents not protect you?"

"They are both dead," I replied. "I have no one whom I can trust."

Suddenly her face relaxed slightly. "Very well, you may join me," she said, and lifting the tray, she marched downstairs again. I followed as she led the way down a further flight to the basement kitchen.

"There are far too many stairs in this house," she grumbled. "It needs several domestics to keep it as it should be kept."

I turned as we went into the kitchen, and said sincerely, "How homelike this is."

A fire burned cheerfully in the huge stove, the curtains and rug were bright red, and comfortable chairs were drawn up by the fire. Everything was spotlessly clean, and the brass and copper pans and jugs twinkled in the firelight. Otherwise it was rather poorly lighted, as not a great deal of light came in the basement windows, but one soon grew accustomed to it.

A small white cloth was laid at one end of the big scrubbed table, and Frau Kramper quickly set another place, and we started our first meal together. She was not exactly communicative, but at least she was less hostile.

Sensing that she would think it beneath her dignity to question me, I gave her a brief explanation of why I had come to work in Geneva, and why I had been so desirous of finding another job and residence.

She listened with scarcely a word, and I wondered if she believed me; then as the bell above the door rang, she hurried upstairs.

When she came down again, she said as she unloaded the tray she carried, "Monsieur Poitier says you are free now for two hours. You must go out for exercise."

"I would rather not," I replied. "I am afraid Edo, or others, may search for me."

"Very well, then I will accompany you," she replied. "We will go by paths where they will be unlikely to think of looking."

"But you need rest," I said.

"Fiddlesticks, I am not an old woman yet."

"Then I will help you with the dishes," I insisted, and I believe that gesture finally made Frau Kramper my friend.

"There is no need," she said grumpily, but picking up the drying cloth, I proceeded to make myself useful.

From then on, for about an hour every afternoon, Frau Kramper insisted on accompanying me along the country paths away from the town. I never went into Geneva. If I needed anything, Frau Kramper shopped for me, and gradually my fears of being discovered, subsided.

I had written to my aunt, explaining why I had been forced to move from Marie's home, telling her of my present employment and of the care Frau Kramper took of me. This, I knew, would allay her anxiety; and I begged her not to give my address to her husband, or to Marie, if she wrote inquiring where I was. I hoped that in time, Marie and her family would assume that I had left Geneva.

I often smiled to myself, as I thought what a strange pair Frau Kramper and I must have made as we set out every afternoon.

I was much taller than she was, with her typically solid German figure. She always wore a wide-brimmed, black felt hat, screwed on to her big bun of hair with a large steel hatpin. Her skirts were wide and trailing, her boots flat-heeled and clumsily made. She strode along, putting her feet down heavily with the toes turning outward at a wide angle; and always she carried a long rusty-black umbrella, which she plonked down with a vicious prod at every step.

She talked in Low German, and at first I found it difficult to follow. I could speak Swiss French, and Swiss German, but this was rather different. Obviously, Frau Kramper was glad to have someone who knew her own language more than most of the people in Geneva did, and years later I was to be thankful to her for that practice.

After our brisk walk, she ordered me to rest for an hour; then at about four o'clock, I was given a cup of coffee and a pastry, and allowed to work again until seven o'clock.

Often I worked alone in the study, laboriously copying the sheaves of papers, which mounted day by day. Sometimes Monsieur Poitier worked at his desk for hours without speaking; sometimes he was out most of the day, copying down data he required in the library.

I realized that he must often work into the early hours of the morning, because when I went to bed, I could still see the light from the study window streaming out across the small garden in front of the house.

We had so little to say to each other; yet I felt a sense

of peace and security in this house, such as I had not experienced for a long time.

Frau Kramper never became affectionate, but at least
she ceased to resent my presence, and by gathering a
hint here and there, I pieced her story together. Her
husband had been an engineer, and had been sent to
Geneva to work. Frau Kremper did not like Switzerland,
but when he died in an accident, she was left with three
young children, and as they had already started school
and she had a house, she chose to stay where she was.
Conditions were difficult in Germany in those days, and
she had decided she could support her family by taking
in paying guests during the vacation seasons, when so
many tourists poured into Switzerland.

Then two children died with diphtheria, and she was
left with only her eldest son, Freiderik, who was then
about twelve years old. He was a brilliant boy like his
father, and she determined he would go to the university. To make this possible, she sold their house and took
a job as housekeeper. Freiderik had taken a degree at
Hamburg University, and was now working in Germany.
Always he had said he would make a home for her
when he had finished studying, but now he was married
and did not need her, and she did not want to share a
home with her daughter-in-law. She preferred to be independent, and here in the house of Baroness Wykeham
and Monsieur Poitier, she was almost her own mistress.

Gradually, I noticed a change in Frau Kramper. Her
face looked even more serious, and she spoke less than
ever. After letters from Germany, she seemed unsettled;
and I noticed that every morning she seized the newspaper even before Monsieur Poitier had opened it, and
scanned the headlines with an anxious frown on her
brow.

Occasionally, too, Monsieur Poitier would sigh as he
glanced at the news; and sometimes he said sadly, "The
war clouds are gathering again. Why must men try to
destroy each other?"

I understood very little of the political conditions of
the world at that time. Shut away in this little backwa-

ter, I was content to go on day by day, thankful for the peace and security that surrounded me.

I dreaded the thought of the return of the baroness. Perhaps she would object to my living in the house. Perhaps, like others, she would resent me and insist that I leave this home, which I had come to love in so short a time.

My pile of clearly-written pages grew higher and higher, and often Monsieur Poitier gave me other work to copy and letters to write. Nowadays, of course I would have a typewriter, but at that time, handcopying was more widely used.

As the days went by, even in this quiet house, a feeling of tension crept in. The baroness was detained in England longer than she expected, as there were many technical difficulties over legal settlements. She had written, urging her stepson to join her, but he said he preferred to stay until his book was finished.

From Frau Kramper, I had learned that my employer was the son of a French diplomat who had married an Arabian girl. She had died when Pierre, their first baby, was born, and later his father had married Lady Margaret Wykeham, whom Frau Kramper always called "the baroness." She had brought Pierre up as her own son, and after the death of his father, had brought the boy to Europe. He had gone to various schools in France, Italy, England, and Spain—anywhere the baroness had settled for any length of time. She had money of her own and kept Pierre well supplied. He was not strong, and had had several spells of treatment in sanatoriums. That was why they had come to Switzerland. Pierre loved to study, and he had been working on his book for many months.

At that time, Geneva was full of foreigners studying at the university, besides the continual flow of tourists; and it soon became obvious that the police were scanning all outsiders very carefully. Everyone had to go to the security office to be questioned and to register. As I was a Swiss citizen, I had no trouble, but Pierre and

Frau Kramper were aliens, and were regarded as potential spies or troublemakers.

One day Frau Kramper startled us by announcing that she was leaving immediately for Germany. Her son had sent her the money, and insisted that she leave at once, and Monsieur Poitier seemed to understand, for he made no objection. Later he explained that he felt war was imminent, and it was as well for people to return to their own country.

"Will you have to leave?" I asked, my heart heavy with fear.

He smiled rather sadly. "I can hardly claim any country as my own. I have a French passport, but I have never lived long in France. I could go to England to my stepmother, but that country, too, is preparing for war. I cannot fight because of my health, so I will take my chances here. I believe Switzerland will endeavor to stay neutral, so I may be able to escape the terrible holocaust to come."

I let out my breath in relief, then my heart started to beat quickly once more as he said, "But what about you? Without Frau Kramper we will be alone, and that is not suitable for one so young. I was expecting my stepmother any day, but she has met with an accident, and has a broken leg, so she cannot travel at present."

"Please let me stay," I begged. "You will need someone to look after the house and cook your meals when Frau Kramper has gone."

"I must advertise for another housekeeper. Have you no friends to whom you can go, or a friend who could come here to stay in the meantime?"

"There is no one I would trust," I replied.

"I have often gone to the bookstore where you used to work, and have heard that the brother who annoyed you has been called into the army, so at least you are safe from his persecution. Marie, your friend, is taking nursing training, but I admit I do not care for the other sister, or her so-called boyfriend. I will go to the employment office today and try to replace Frau Kramper."

Frau Kramper departed, and I was surprised at how upset I was to see her go. She had been good to me in her own way, and had helped me to grow a little more sure of myself.

Monsieur Poitier returned with the news that there was no housekeeper available. The hotels were full of people pouring into what they hoped was the comparative safety of Switzerland. A woman would come in during the day to clean, but it was impossible to find someone willing to sleep in the house.

This did not worry me, because I felt I could trust Monsieur Poitier implicitly. Never by word or action had he given me the slightest indication that he thought of me as an attractive woman, and my greatest worry was that he might have to leave the country, and I would be homeless once more.

I was too young to realize that I had fallen in love with my employer. I knew that I admired and respected him, but I thought of him as being far above me in every way. If only I could stay in his home and serve him, I believed I would be completely satisfied. He was about thirty years old, a man of learning who had traveled widely. To him, I was sure, I was only a young, uninformed, simple girl. I had nothing to offer such a man, except a willingness to serve him in any capacity I could.

## 2

FIVE DAYS after Frau Kramper left, World War One was declared, and from then on, the peaceful interlude I had been enjoying was shattered.

The woman who was to come in each day, sent a note saying that she and her family were moving back to her father-in-law's farm, and we knew it was useless to look further for help. For the time being, everything was in chaos.

I was able to spend less time in the study, as I had to care for the house, cook the meals, and do the shopping. Monsieur Poitier did not go out much; but when he did, he came back looking very serious. I was too shy to ask questions; and with the departure of Frau Kramper, my employer seemed to have changed toward me. When he spoke to me, I noticed that he seldom met my eyes; it was as if he had erected a barrier between us.

Once or twice he had suggested tentatively that this was not the sort of life I ought to have, and he would understand if I wanted to move to more exciting employment. I wondered if he was trying to get rid of me. Was he short of money? Was he only keeping me out of kindness?

I noticed that he did not look well, and wondered if the old weakness was recurring. He ate very little; and sometimes I could hear him moving about late into the night, when he ought to have been resting. I cooked all the tempting dishes I knew, and did everything I could for his comfort; but still he seemed depressed. He mentioned once that his stepmother was pressing him to try to reach her in England, and I became obsessed with the idea that he wanted to get rid of me. Perhaps I was being a burden to him.

One night, it was so hot that I could not sleep. The clock struck hour after hour, until I felt I must have some fresh air. Throwing on a light wrap, I crept down to the lounge and opened the big window to let the night air blowing from the lake cool my aching head.

I did not switch on the light, as the room was illuminated by the lamps along the quay and the moonlight. I pulled a chair to the window and stared out for a long time; then feeling suddenly overcome by a sense of loneliness and a longing for something I could not define, the tears ran down my cheeks and I began to sob.

Suddenly I felt arms go around my shoulders, and a gentle voice said, "My darling, what has upset you? Why are you so unhappy?"

Turning, I looked into his beautiful dark eyes, and there read something which made my heart pound and my tears stop.

"I'm so afraid you will send me away."

"I could more easily cut off my right arm," he said gently. "Has it not occurred to you that you mean more to me now than life itself? But am I doing right in letting you stay here with me? I am so much older than you are, and a sick man into the bargain, while you are young and beautiful, with all your life before you."

"All I want is to be with you," I said humbly.

"I love you, Annalisa. I want to marry you at once and have the right to care for you."

"But you are learned, and so much more educated than I am," I faltered. "All I have to give you is my love."

He took me in his arms then; and for a while, it was as if the world stood still.

At length he said, "I will write to my stepmother tomorrow and tell her of our love, and that I wish to marry you. Although I am grown up, she still has charge of the money my father left, and I am dependent on her. She has been a wonderful mother to me, but I feel she still thinks of me as a child."

"Perhaps she will not allow you to marry me," I said.

"As soon as she meets you, she will love you also," Pierre replied, but I wondered if he really felt as certain as he tried to sound.

"I'm not of age, so I can't marry you without my guardian's consent," I said. "I don't want her husband to know where I am."

"I will write to her tomorrow," Pierre insisted. "If necessary we will go to visit her, so that I can show her that I only desire your happiness."

The moon had disappeared, and dawn was breaking when we finally separated, but my mind was in far too great a turmoil to rest. I could scarcely believe this wonderful thing which had come to me. I thought I knew why I had been restless and uncertain. All the love of my heart was given to Pierre, and whatever the future held for us, no one could take away the joy and wonder of the revelation that he returned my love.

The next day, our letters were written, and we waited impatiently for the replies. Although not my legal guardian, my uncle refused his consent and ordered me to return to his house immediately, but my aunt had also written separately and told me that on no account must I do so. She believed her husband's mind was becoming deranged, and she was afraid he would harm someone seriously during one of his terrible rages. She sent her written consent, so at least I was free to marry Pierre without waiting until my twenty-first birthday, which was still several months away.

Pierre heard from the baroness. She would not give him permission to marry me; and she threatened to cut off his allowance, if he persisted in having me in his house.

We were obsessed with the sense that our happiness would not last, and I longed to feel that we really belonged to each other.

Pierre talked often with me now and explained much of the world situation that I had never understood before. Everywhere, even in Switzerland, there was danger; and we were afraid something would happen to separate us.

He explained that for centuries, Geneva had been a sort of "city of refuge." In the sixteenth century, thousands of English, Italian, and Spanish Protestants had fled from the Inquisition; later came the Huguenots; and now thousands were pouring in because they believed Switzerland would remain neutral. Here were the headquarters of the international committee of the red cross, started in 1863 by a Genevan, Henri Durant, because he had been so shocked by the sufferings of soldiers in battle.

I knew that all our men had to train with the militia from the age of twenty to fifty for several weeks of the

year, and that we had a strong fighting force, ready at
any moment to fight for our little country. Years ago,
our superbly trained fighting men used to act as merce-
naries, or hired soldiers, in the armies of other European countries. Now the Swiss Guard at the Vatican was
all that remained of that practice. Not since the Napo-
leonic wars had Switzerland actually been involved in
armed conflict. With the Alps making a natural fortress,
and a well-trained army ever ready, it had been able to
maintain its neutrality.

It was a hard situation. Pierre and I loved each other
so much, and we were alone in the house day and night.
Such a situation always puts unbearable pressure upon
two people so deeply in love. At last, Pierre gave in to
my pleading, and we were married very quietly, as neither of us had friends we wanted to invite. Also, Pierre
did not want his mother to know until she returned to
Switzerland.

We were not left in peace for long. One day, a man
came to interview Pierre and ordered him to accompany
him to the security office.

All day, I waited alone, imagining what was happening. I knew if Pierre had been released, he would hurry
back to comfort me, but I had heard so many stories
lately of people disappearing, and no one knowing
where they had gone.

Late at night, I heard voices. The bell rang, but I was
afraid to answer it, then I heard Pierre's voice telling me
to open the door. There were four men with him, and
two of them took me by the arms and led me into the
nearest room.

"We are from the police," they said politely. "There's
no need for you to be alarmed. We have orders to
search the house, but we will not damage anything."

Switzerland was, at that time, a nest of spies from every part of the world, and the federal police often
searched hotels and private houses where strangers and
foreigners were living. I thought at first it was a routine
visit for security reasons, but they asked me many ques-

tions, including where I came from, why I was in Geneva, if I was Pierre's wife, and so on.

I told them I was his secretary, but I was sure now that the visit was the result of information sent by my uncle.

At last two of them departed, taking Pierre with them, and I was left with the other two on guard.

In his first letter, Pierre told me he was being kept under preventative police observation until they had received news concerning him from his own country. "I will be released in a few days," he wrote cheerfully. "Wait quietly until I come back to you."

The two police guards watched my every movement; and when I went to the market, one followed behind me. They had orders to arrest every visitor who came to the house, but Pierre had no close friends in Geneva. He and his stepmother had not lived there long enough to have entered into the social life.

As the days passed, I had nothing to do. Pierre's book was finished, and I began to feel I would go crazy if I had to stay alone all day. The police guard left, and I had no one to talk to. Pierre wrote, urging me to go back to my friends if I could, but what was life without him? He had left me a little money, and my needs were small. The house belonged to his stepmother, so at least I had a roof over my head, and I could keep it in order, ready for Pierre's return.

Everyone was being urged to train for one of the social services, so eventually I went to a Red Cross school, and tried to forget some of my misery in studying.

Ever since I was a child, I had longed to be a doctor. Because I had seen how my aunt suffered in the limitations caused by polio, I had made up my mind that if possible, I would do what I could to help people who suffered. I was interested in everything I could learn in these lectures, and took books home to study.

One of the teaching doctors was immensely popular with the other would-be nurses. He was tall and very well mannered, and the girls made no secret of their admiration. I was interested in his lectures, but the man himself did not attract me. I loved Pierre and had thoughts for no one else.

Three months after I started training, I had a formal proposal of marriage from this doctor. I was dumb-founded, for he had never singled me out, or shown unusual interest in me.

If I had not met Pierre, what a temptation this would have been. But Pierre needed me; someday he would be free, and my love would make up to him for what he was suffering now.

Three days later, Pierre was released, but he was a sick man. Now all I wanted to do was to nurse him back to health. That night, like two frightened children, we slept in each other's arms.

I wrote again to my aunt, but there was no reply. There was a letter from Pierre's stepmother; but after reading it, he tore it up and did not tell me what was in it.

Gradually, Pierre grew stronger, and we tried to find what happiness we could. Then I began to notice that he ate very little, and never suggested that we go out for an occasional meal, even to the cheapest cafe. I worried about him, trying to tempt him, but he insisted that all he wanted was coffee.

One day after he had been out alone, I saw that his golden watch chain, his valuable shirt buttons, and his cuff links were missing.

Then I began to understand. He had had to sell these things because there was no more money coming from his stepmother.

I realized then that all I had brought to him was poverty and an uncertain future. Would it be better for him if I went away and left him alone? But who would care for him, sick as he was?

He was so feverish that I sent for a doctor, and he ordered at least a month of treatment in a mountain sanatorium; but how was this to be managed, when we had no money?

All I had was my mother's jewelry, and into my mind

came my aunt's words, "Someday you may be in desperate need." What more desperate need could there be than this?

Eventually I managed to get two thousand francs for them—a large sum at that time.

When I told him that the doctor had made arrangements for him to enter the sanatorium, Pierre said, "I cannot go, we have no money to pay the fees."

"They are already paid," I replied. "You have no need to worry."

He stared at me, then getting up, went to the drawer where I had kept the jewelry. The box was empty, and with eyes filled with tears, he said, "I cannot let you do this, my darling. Someday you may need that money for yourself."

"You are more important than anything else in life," I replied.

"Someday, please God, I will make it up to you, beloved," he said, taking me in his arms.

That night, I had a hard battle with myself. I knew now that I was carrying Pierre's baby. Should I tell him? Was he in a fit state to have this extra worry thrust upon him? When he recovered, it would be time enough to tell him. In the meantime, I would hug the secret to myself. I would have to find employment of some sort to help keep myself, and save a little toward the future.

The day after Pierre departed, a newspaper agency offered me a job as a translator, and I was happy to accept. They had learned of my knowledge of languages from pamphlets I had translated for Pierre some months ago.

How I missed Pierre in the days that followed. His letters came regularly, and I know he tried to write cheerfully for my sake; but I could sense that at present there was little improvement in his health, and I wondered what he would do if the money I had obtained for the jewelry did not hold out. Surely Pierre's stepmother would not refuse to help with his treatment, especially if he did not tell her he had married me. This made it even more imperative for me to keep the coming baby a secret, even though I believed Pierre would be as pleased about it as I was. Whatever happened, I could not regret it. Always I would have some part of Pierre left to me.

## 3

AMONG THOSE who worked in the newspaper office was a journalist called Hans Fischer, who had one of the most ugly faces I had ever seen. I felt sorry for him, even while his looks repelled me. No one liked him, and he was left very much alone. I thought it was because of his ugliness, and so I tried to be pleasant. In return he helped me with my work, and as he lived in the same direction as I did, he often accompanied me home.

He told me about a girl he had loved, but she had laughed at his love. Because I was so lonely, and I believed he was a friend whom I could trust, I told him my story. I told Pierre about this man in my letters, and he was glad I had someone to befriend me.

His letters were loving and tender and full of hope, but the weeks went by without any word of his return. Soon it would be impossible to hide my condition any longer.

One morning before leaving for work, I was handed a card requesting me to go to the office of the chief of police, as they required certain information. What did they want from me? Was there more trouble ahead for Pierre? I confided my fears to Hans, and he promised to accompany me.

"Let me handle this myself," he said kindly. "I will see that there is no trouble for you."

To my surprise, when the police chief began to question me, Hans said I was his fiancée, and demanded to know the meaning of this interrogation. I was a Swiss citizen; why then was I being treated like this?

The chief looked from one to the other in perplexity, then pulled out a letter and read it. Eventually he said, "I am sorry, there must have been a mistake; this is not the young lady who ought to have been interviewed. Please accept my apologies."

Back on the street, with my heart beating normally once more, I tried to put my relief and thanks into words, but still the thought persisted that somehow this interview meant further danger.

Hans put his hand on my arm. "I need no thanks," he said, with a smile which was meant to be pleasant. "What I told the chief of police was true. I meant it. I love you and will protect you always, as I did this morning."

I pulled away from his hand, all the color draining from my face. "You know that I am married to Pierre, that whatever happens, I belong to him," I said angrily.

"You will never be able to live together again," he said. "Do you not understand that he is a foreigner, and that he is dying? You are in love with a dream. Your Pierre will never make a home for you, because he is under police surveillance, and when he is well enough will go to prison, or be forced to leave the country. We do not trust men such as he these days."

"How can you be so cruel?" I cried.

"I'm not cruel. What I'm telling you is for your own happiness. Think of the child you are carrying. I will love him better than any of my own, because I have sworn never to create another being with such an ugly face as mine. Give me your child. I will care for both of you. Come with me to my home, and when you are free, we will be married, and I will adopt your child."

"I must have time to think," I said to gain time. Never would I give my child to such a father. I would rather kill myself and the unborn baby than let that happen.

"I will have everything ready for you," he said. "You must realize, when you think it over, that I am offering you a home and a Swiss name for your child."

"Yes, I must think it over," I agreed, and hurried into the office.

How I got through my work that day, I do not know, but I took care that I did not have to accompany Hans Fischer on my way home.

Early the next morning, I sent a telegram to Pierre, and left Geneva by the first train. We met at the Lausanne station, then together traveled to Berne. Now I could keep my secret from Pierre no longer, and in spite of our problems, we rejoiced in this even stronger bond between us.

We went together to a lawyer, Monsieur Shaffner, and explained our situation. He said he would write to the baroness, but for the present, Pierre must continue with his treatment.

Almost another month passed. I was living in a women's hostel, Pierre in a sanatorium, but we could meet often and comfort each other.

One afternoon I was going to the post office to see if there was any mail for us, when I suddenly halted with shock. Hans Fischer was coming down the stairs of the post office building! There was no mistaking his grotesque face and almost square figure.

He had not seen me, so I slipped quickly through a door which led into a courtyard, from which I entered a side street, and ran all the way home.

For several days, I was afraid to go out on the streets, and when I was forced to do so, I kept looking around wherever I went. I hoped he had gone back to Geneva, but one evening when I accompanied Pierre to the bus, and was kissing him goodnight, I heard the click of a camera. Looking around, I saw Fischer's horribly grinning face.

"You thought you could fool me," he said, when he had seen Pierre step into the bus. "I haven't finished with you yet," and he disappeared into the crowd.

A few days later, the wonderful news came that Pierre's book was to be published by a French publisher, and that the baroness had agreed to our marriage.

Pierre's stepmother had deposited a small sum of money for his use for medical treatment and traveling expenses. She had asked Monsieur Shaffner to arrange for passports for both of us to come to England. It seemed to Pierre and me that at last there was a glimmer of light at the end of the dark tunnel through which we had been struggling.

That evening, we went out to dine in celebration. We could only afford the very cheapest of food, but how happy we were.

Two days later, I waited for Pierre at the usual place, but he did not come. I waited four hours, then went back to the hostel to see if he had sent any word. I was afraid he must be ill again, so summoning my courage, I set off for the pension where he was staying.

As soon as the proprietor saw me, he threw up his arms and talked with tears on his cheeks. "Madame, how sorry I am that your husband has gone. He was not allowed time even to write a note, but he asked me to tell you that you must take care of yourself, and he will get in touch with you as soon as possible."

"But what happened?" I gasped.

"The police, you understand. They came early this morning and took him away. They said they were taking him to the French border. He was being expelled from Switzerland for reasons of security."

The awful words "expelled from Switzerland" hammered on my brain, and I felt myself swaying, and the face of Hans Fischer flashed through my mind. He seemed well acquainted with the workings of the police.

When I came around, I was conscious only of waves of pain washing over me; then it seemed that for an endless time, I was dying, and I could hear myself crying out in pain.

When at last I became fully conscious, I found I was in a big room, and a nurse was slapping my face, while a doctor stood watching. Then I was given something to drink, and an injection was put in my arm.

Suddenly I saw another nurse holding a baby upside down, and slapping it until it began to cry. The miracle had happened. That baby was my own—Pierre's and mine—and I held out my arms to clasp him to me.

As I looked down on those tiny features before they took him from me, the tears poured down my face. How Pierre would have loved him, but when would we meet again? He had been sent away, and I had no idea where he had gone, or what was happening to him.

Later I was told that my aunt's address had been found in my handbag, and because the authorities feared I was going to die, they had contacted her. The day after my baby was born, my uncle arrived and insisted that I return to his home as soon as I was strong enough, but I refused to leave Berne. I had to stay where my baby's father could reach me. He became so angry and abusive, that the young lady doctor who had attended me, insisted that he leave, as his visit was upsetting me.

Evidently he arranged an interview with her, and told her a long tale about my ingratitude to himself and his wife. They were willing to take me back and care for the child. I was unfit to be left on my own to get into more trouble.

When I was feeling stronger, the doctor, Margaret Roos, talked to me about my plans for when I left the hospital. She had been very kind, and finally I told her why I refused to go back to my guardian's house. Gradually she drew me out, and longing to confide in some older person, I told her my sad little story. Sometimes I wondered if people would believe me if I told them the truth, but Dr. Roos had evidently learned enough from my unconscious ramblings to know that what I said was true.

"How could your husband get in touch with you?" she asked.

"We have a box number at the post office. He knows I will keep going there. I cannot leave Berne until I hear from him, but somehow I must work and support our baby."

"Have you decided on his name?" she asked.

"It was to be Jean-Pierre if it was a boy," I said with a sob. I was still so weak that tears were always near the surface.

"Try to sleep now," Dr. Roos said quietly. "You must be strong, so that you can feed little Jean-Pierre and take care of him."

Two days later she came to me again and sat down by my bed.

"Annalisa, I have talked to the hospital authorities and told them a little of your story. You have learned some nursing, and we could let you stay in the hospital as a ward orderly, if you would care for the work. It would not be a large salary, but you would have a room and your food."

"But my baby?" I asked. "You would not want to take him from me?"

"You can keep him in your room when off duty and in the nursery when you're working. I warn you that the hours will be long, and the work tiring, and you will be ordered here and there by all and sundry."

Again tears filled my eyes. "How can I thank you for such great kindness?" I said.

She smiled and replied. "You're no ordinary girl, Annalisa; already you have suffered too much."

"Once I longed to be a doctor, so that I'd be able to help others," I said.

Dr. Roos nodded. "Do you believe God will take care of you if you ask Him, Annalisa?"

"I go to church when I can," I replied. "But since my mother died, religion has not meant much to me. Long ago she used to talk to me about Jesus loving me."

"He does love us," Dr. Roos said simply. "He died for you and me, and to realize He knows all about me is the greatest thing in my life."

"I wish I could feel like that," I said wistfully.

From her pocket, she took a small book and handed it to me. "Read this while you have time to think about

it quietly, Annalisa," and with a smile, she hurried
away.

I examined the book and found it was her own copy
of the New Testament, which I had never read before.
My aunt and uncle had been Roman Catholics, and to
them the Bible was a book of heresies. We had to believe what the church and priests taught, but I had never
seen that their religion was any real part of their lives.

Pierre too had been a nominal Roman Catholic, but
only very occasionally had we gone to church on a feast
day, and it had not meant anything to me personally.
God was a being far away from ordinary people, a being
who punished those who did wrong, unless the church
took one under its protection and was paid the money
demanded for its services. It had never entered my adult
mind that God knew anything about an ordinary girl
like Annalisa Poitier.

For hours I read the book Dr. Roos had given me.
Some of the parables and stories I remembered my
mother telling me, and I remembered now that she had
taken me sometimes to a small Protestant chapel, but
my father had been angry when she did so, and there
had been long arguments about it. Since her death, I
had simply accepted what I was taught by the priests
and the nuns, who were our teachers in the schools I attended.

Dr. Roos talked to me when she had a spare moment,
but the hospital was busy, and she began to look very
weary. I enjoyed reading the gospels and acts, but after
that I got very muddled. I had no one to explain what it
was all about, and although I enjoyed much of the majesty of the language, I did not understand what it meant.

Gradually I was allowed out of bed; then for two
weeks I was sent with my baby to a small convalescent
home in the mountains, but I was in a fever to come
back to see if there was any word from Pierre. Dr. Roos
had promised that she would visit the post office and inquire at the box number, but no word came from her.

When I returned to the hospital, to a small room on
the staff corridor, there was still no news, and as day

followed day, my heart became heavier and my outlook more hopeless. The work was hard, and not everyone was pleasant. Often I had to endure hints and slights from those with whom I worked; and because people believed that I was an unmarried mother, some of the men obviously thought I was fair game and would welcome their attentions.

Jean-Pierre was fretful at night and cried most of the day. He did not gain weight, and eventually Dr. Roos said I must wean him, as it was obvious I had no nourishment for him.

"You are worrying, Annalisa, and that is the worst thing you can do for your baby. Also, I realize the work is hard, so we will try bottle-feeding."

From that time, he began to improve; and soon he was sleeping well, and taking all the milk he could get, and looking for more.

Dr. Roos moved to another hospital, and with her going, I felt my only friend had deserted me. She had been completing her training, and was now going on to a more senior position.

"I'll continue to pray for you, Annalisa," she said, when she managed to find me alone for a few moments. "Keep the New Testament, and promise me you'll go on reading it. If you're in need of help, this address will always reach me. I'll be glad to hear how Jean-Pierre is growing, so write to me when you can."

"I will never forget your kindness," I said brokenly. "You have shown God's love to me, and made me believe that everyone is not evil or unkind."

"Perhaps I'll be able to hear of an easier job for you, but I realize you don't want to leave Berne. Don't give up hope. During war, letters go astray, or people are not allowed to write."

"I'm afraid something serious must have happened," I said, only too relieved to be able to tell another human being of my continual fears. "Pierre was a sick man; he was not strong enough to stand privation and hardship; and France is in the grip of war. He could be in prison, if not already dead."

"Why not write to his stepmother?"

"I already have."

"Then you know her address?"

"I know where Pierre used to write."

"Tell me. Perhaps I may be able to get in touch with her."

"Lady Mary Wykeham, Wykeham Manor, Leicestershire," I recited, writing it down on a piece of paper. "Surely she would have replied if she had received my letter."

"Write again," she suggested. "As I said, letters go so easily astray during wartime; or she may have moved to another home since you had that address."

Some days later, feeling desperate with uncertainty, I went to see Monsieur Shaffner, the lawyer whom Pierre and I had consulted. He received me kindly and told me that there was still some money standing to Pierre's account. If I needed it badly, he would hand it over to Pierre's son. He promised to write to Lady Mary, and he would let me know as soon as he had a reply.

Then one day, when I had a few hours off, I dressed Jean-Pierre and bought a ticket to Geneva. What I hoped to find, I did not really know, but I longed to see the place where Pierre and I had had our great happiness.

When I approached the house, a further shock awaited me. A notice outside proclaimed that this was the Bureau of the Office of Food. Nothing of Pierre or the baroness remained. It had been the property of foreigners, so the Swiss government had simply requisitioned it.

I made my way back to the station, then to the hospital, my arms aching with Jean-Pierre's weight; but this was nothing, compared to the despair in my heart. I had no idea where else I could turn. I had tried everything I could think of, and now I was certain that Pierre must be dead. Otherwise I was sure that somehow he would have communicated with me.

I received a letter from Monsieur Shaffner, saying that the only news he could obtain was that Lady Mary was engaged in some sort of war work, and had left England, but no one seemed certain of her whereabouts.

My aunt died, and my uncle again invited me to return home. His son was married, and he was now alone. He promised that he would respect my wishes and provide for my baby, but I did not even trouble to reply. There was also a letter and a small parcel forwarded after my aunt's death, which her husband obviously knew nothing about. In it, she enclosed some small pieces of jewelry and some money.

She wrote,

> This is all the money I have managed to save secretly. It is yours, Annalisa. There ought to have been more from what your father left in trust for you, but when I mention it, your uncle flies into such a rage that I am afraid he will kill me. I wish I could have seen you and the baby. I know I have very little time left now, and I will be glad to be at peace. God has comforted me these last years, and I have drawn near to Him. I pray that our Saviour will receive my soul when I die. I have prayed often for you, that you will be happy, and that Pierre may be restored to you. This terrible war has brought such untold suffering; surely it can only be the power of the evil one, who is seeking to destroy all that is good. If you never see your Pierre again, do not marry only for the sake of your baby. I married without love, because the one I loved had died, but you know the sort of life I have had. Let my story be an example of a loveless marriage. Sexual attraction never lasts, and I know with your beauty, you will always attract men who are unscrupulous.

I wept long over that letter and the pieces of jewelry that night. It seemed that one by one, everybody who had ever shown me love for my own sake was being taken from me. I felt that few girls of twenty-one could be as lonely as I was. The only moments of happiness I had were when I dressed and fed Jean-Pierre and sat with him clasped in my arms. Every time I looked at his little face, the memory of his father deepened the ache in my heart. I could see no resemblance to myself in my baby. He was Pierre's replica in every way. His skin had a smooth, dark texture; his eyes were a velvety brown, and his hair was jet black. I was very fair and had a big frame, but Jean-Pierre had long slender limbs and delicately molded features. To me, no other baby could ever have been so beautiful; but what sort of a life was before him?

As the weeks passed into months, and he developed from a helpless baby into a determined little person with a mind of his own, I began to realize it would be impossible to continue indefinitely in the hospital. As soon as Jean-Pierre was able to run about, I would be unable to leave him in his cot or baby carriage all day. My wages were too small to make any sort of home and pay someone to look after him, even if I could find such a person. Even one room was beyond my finances.

Dr. Roos continued to write to me; in fact, at that time she was my only correspondent. Sometimes she sent me gifts of clothes for Jean-Pierre, and I was grateful, as he was growing so fast. She sent clothes for me also, and I treasured them, not knowing what was before me. I considered them too good to work in; and apart from wheeling Jean-Pierre out for an hour each afternoon when I was off duty, I went nowhere. She often put little thoughts about God and His love in her letters, but I felt far too bitter to believe anything.

If God had loved me, he would not have taken Pierre from me and our defenseless baby. To me, God was a cruel, relentless being.

Terrible stories of the atrocities of war drifted into the hospital, stories of hundreds of innocent women and children who had been caught up in this horrible maelstrom of madness. Thousands were homeless and were dying of starvation and disease; thousands were being driven into labor camps; untold numbers had disappeared, and no one knew what had happened to them.

Night after night, I thought of Pierre being sent to a

country where he had no home and no resources. Had he been captured and thrown into prison, or shot down by enemy bullets, or had he died of cold and starvation? His constitution would never stand up to hiding in ditches or going without food. Sometimes in the midst of my bitterness, I would chide myself with the thought that there were others far worse off than I was. At least I had a roof over my head and food to eat, even though rationing was making its restrictions very evident, and I had my baby with me. He was well and strong and growing more adorable every day. Many mothers had been separated from their children or had been forced to watch them die before their very eyes, while I, at least, had my child to comfort me.

WHEN JEAN-PIERRE was a year old, Margaret Roos found a place for me in the home of another doctor. His wife had several children and needed help, so they were willing to allow my baby to live with me.

If work in the hospital was hard, this was far worse. There, we had had regular hours off duty, but in the home of Dr. Demmer, it was work from early morning until late at night. Madame Demmer imagined herself a semi-invalid, and never exerted herself. The children were undisciplined and precocious. I soon found I was expected to take the whole responsibility for the family of five, do all the housework, laundry, cooking, and answer the door to patients. I had no time to spend on Jean-Pierre, and his life became a very haphazard affair. Sometimes the older children would be kind to him, sometimes tease and annoy him. Walter, the two-year old, was jealous of any attention paid to the younger child.

My wages were small, because Madame Demmer said providing for Jean-Pierre accounted for part of it. I tried desperately to save for the future, but my tiny hoard mounted very slowly. I grew more and more tired, and my patience was tried beyond endurance day after day. I lost a lot of weight, and one day even Dr. Demmer noticed my pallor, and issued to me a bottle of tonic.

I realized that I could not go on this way much longer, and began secretly searching in discarded newspapers for advertisements for housekeepers. I applied for several, but either there was no reply, or the answer was that the advertiser could not consider having a young child in the home to take up my time.

I was growing desperate, and was almost at the point of applying to Margaret Roos for help, when a letter came from my mother's brother in Italy. I never found out how he had traced me, but perhaps my uncle or aunt had given him my address.

I could only remember Uncle Ernst and Aunt Rita very slightly. Once when I was a child, they had come to visit my parents. Uncle Ernst was my mother's only brother, and had gone to work in Italy as a young man. There he had married Rita and settled down. I remembered him as a big, fair man with a hearty laugh, who was very kind to me. Aunt Rita had been small and dark, and chattered in a language I couldn't understand. Then, they had had two small children, Giovanni and Lucia, but I could remember very little about that visit; and since my mother died, I had heard nothing from them.

Now, for some reason, they were writing to inquire of my whereabouts. To me, this letter came as if in answer to my desperate prayers for help. I could hardly wait until everyone was in bed that night, and I could clamber wearily up to my attic bedroom, and exhausted as I was, write to Uncle Ernst. I told him how grateful I was for his letter, as I was so alone, with no one who cared about me. Then I told them about Pierre and my baby, and that I felt sure after all this time that Pierre was dead. I did not ask for help, because it never occurred to me that Uncle Ernst was in a position to help me. I knew he had a large family, and I knew also that life was hard and for the most part, the people very poor in Italy. Next morning I went shopping and posted my letter. The thought that somewhere in the world there was someone who even remembered my existence, made a little warm glow in my heart.

A week later, I received a letter from the lawyer who had tried to contact Lady Mary Wykeham, asking me to call at his office. This faced me with a problem. I had no hours off duty, and I had no wish to tell Madame Demmer anything about this letter. That afternoon, however, she announced that she was going the next day to visit her mother, who lived in Lausanne, and she would be gone for three days. She would take the two youngest children with her. That left me with the three older ones and Jean-Pierre. I would have to take all of them into town with me. Perhaps I could leave them in the waiting room while I went inside.

Next day, I dressed myself as carefully as possible in clothes Dr. Margaret Roos had sent me, got the children ready, and promising them ice cream and lemonade, we took a tramcar into town.

My heart was beating wildly as I shepherded the children into the building, then asked a girl clerk if they could sit down while I visited Monsieur Shaffner. She nodded, and I put Jean-Pierre in Marta's care.

My head was aching violently, as I had had no sleep the night before. My thoughts had gone around and around, hoping that this call meant good news, that at last I was going to hear from Pierre; then again I was weighed down with an awful depression.

Monsieur Shaffner greeted me kindly and begged me to be seated. He looked at me closely, saying, "You do not look so well as when I last saw you. Are you finding the work you are doing too hard?"

My eyes filled at the sympathy in his voice, but I tried to speak calmly. "The hours are very long, but I have been unable to find other employment." Then, unable to contain myself any longer, I burst out, "Have you news for me, Monsieur Shaffner?"

"Let me offer you some wine," he said, and going to a cupboard, he poured out a glass of rich red liquid.

"Drink that, you look as if you need it," he said, and waited while I obediently swallowed it. I felt it warm me, and calm my throbbing head.

"Thank you, I feel that has done me good," I said putting down the empty glass.

Monsieur Shaffner went around to the other side of the large desk, sat down, and shuffled some papers, while I felt I would scream if I had to wait much longer.

At last he coughed, cleared his throat, then said, "I am afraid I have bad news for you. Lady Mary Wykeham has been killed."

"But what about my husband?" I demanded.

"He too is dead," came the quiet, dry announcement.

I stared at his face, too shocked even after all the times I had told myself this, to believe it. Now I realized that all these long months I had been living on hope. In the depth of my mind, I had believed that someday Pierre would come back to me and to little Jean-Pierre. Now the cold, icy hand of finality clutched at my heart.

"When, and how did it happen?" I asked, and was amazed that my voice was so emotionless.

"I told you that all the news I could ascertain was that Lady Mary had gone abroad on war work. Now I have learned that she went to France to find her stepson. Somehow, she had been informed that he had been expelled from Switzerland, and had been left at the French border. She tried by every means possible to locate him, then eventually found him in a hospital in England. He had been captured by the Germans and taken to a prisoner-of-war camp, because he was wearing a military uniform that he had taken from a dead soldier. From that camp, he eventually made his escape, reached the English lines more dead than alive, and was taken to

England, but died two days later. He had managed to give Lady Mary's name, and she was sent for, but arrived too late. Then, I believe, she was trying to reach you; but she was killed on her way to Switzerland, when the train in which she was traveling was destroyed by the enemy."

I had nothing to say. My world was even more empty and lonely. I realized that hope had always been there to keep me going. Now I was truly alone. Jean-Pierre would never see his father. What was there before me, but a life of hard work and loneliness?

Then I became conscious that Monsieur Shaffner was still speaking. "Perhaps we could put in a claim for your son. Lady Mary's title of course dies with her, but there may be money left in her will. I will write to Lady Mary's English lawyer to make inquiries. I will do all that I can to help you, Madame Poitier."

"Thank you," I said, feeling now that I could stand very little more.

"I will get in touch with you as soon as I have further news," he said, as I made for the door.

"You are very kind," I managed to say. "For myself I want nothing; but Pierre would have wanted his child to be provided for, I know."

I stumbled outside, and the children rushed to meet me. I could see that Jean-Pierre had been crying, and my heart ached for him. He was so sweet and so delicately formed, compared with these ordinary, undisciplined, ill-mannered children. I must somehow take him away, so that he would not be brought up in such an atmosphere.

"Now we'll have the ice cream and lemonade you promised," Raoul shouted and tugged at my arm.

"Come, Jean-Pierre," I said, and lifted him in my arms, longing to feel the warmth and comfort of his little body.

"He's a crybaby," Rudy said scoffingly. "He's too big to be carried. Mamma says you will make a softie of him. Walter is only a little older than Jean-Pierre, but he is far bigger and stronger."

I set my lips firmly and made no reply. Now that I knew Pierre would never come back to Berne, I did not need to wait there for his return or for news of him. It no longer mattered where I went. Perhaps I could find some quiet place in the country where I could work and bring up Jean-Pierre.

I could do secretarial work and nursing, but the problem was a home. Until Jean-Pierre was old enough to start school, I must find employment where a home would be provided, so that he could be with me all day.

I begrudged the precious money I had to waste on ice cream and drinks; but I had promised, so there was no getting out of my obligation; but as quickly as I could, I shepherded my little flock back to the place which was the only sort of home I had.

With my mind only half on my tasks that night, I thought and planned. Even the Demmer children realized that I was in no mood to be trifled with, and finally they consented to settle down. Then, when the house was quiet, I wrote to Dr. Margaret and to Uncle Ernst, telling them of the news I had received. I made no mention of the lawyer's idea of inquiring about money, because I had no hope that anyone would bother about a little Swiss boy, unless Pierre or Lady Mary had left a will; and I did not believe Pierre had had the opportunity to do such a thing. Neither he nor Lady Mary had heard of the actual birth of Jean-Pierre, and Pierre was only her stepson.

As the days dragged on, I felt more and more desperate. Hope was dead; and if it had not been for my little Jean-Pierre, I would gladly have put an end to my life. I found it almost a physical pain to drag myself out of bed in the morning; yet when I sank into bed at night, I was too tired to sleep.

Dr. Margaret wrote, saying she was going to call to see me on her next free day; but before that, matters were taken out of my hands.

One morning I struggled up, but could scarcely stand. All day I had spasms of dizziness and had to cling to chairs or tables until the feeling passed. I was trying to serve the evening meal, when I felt myself falling, and had a hazy sense of the children screaming; then I knew nothing more.

When I eventually came to, I thought I was dreaming, for I was once more back in the hospital, the same hospital where Jean-Pierre was born and where I had worked for so long.

I opened my eyes, but the pain caused by the light made me close them again, and I must have floated back into unconsciousness. Then later I heard, as from a great distance, a voice say, "Is there no sign of a return to consciousness yet?"

I lifted my eyelids with a great effort, then closed them again and tried to move my hand.

"Can you hear me, Annalisa?" a voice said gently, close to my ear, and I managed to move my head slightly.

A cool hand held my wrist, and I felt fingers lift my eyelids and peer into my eyes.

After what seemed an endless time, another voice said, "Will you try to drink this?" and a tube was put between my lips which felt dry and cracked.

I swallowed once or twice, then I could not even make the slight effort to suck.

"Very well, go to sleep again," a masculine voice said, and how gladly I felt myself falling once more into the well of dark mistiness.

When I awakened, I knew that I was stronger, for I was able to keep my eyes open, and I saw that a young nurse was sitting by my bed.

"Awake at last," she said with a smile. "You've certainly had a long sleep. Now perhaps you can have something to eat."

She pressed a bell by the bed, and a nun hurried in.

"Awake? Good. Now we will freshen you up and make you comfortable."

Very gently they wiped my face and hands, changed my sheets, then again offered me food through a feeding tube

"There now, you are ready to see our favorite doctor," the sister said cheerfully. I was so tired that I could not speak or even smile. All I wanted was to sink back into that black oblivion.

Dr. Jaeggi hurried in and began the usual routine with his stethoscope, while the sister watched his every movement.

At last he nodded his head, turned away, and in a low voice talked to the sister at the other side of the screen, but I was too exhausted to feel any interest in what he said.

"We want to give you a little prick, then you must sleep again," the sister said when she returned, and a moment later I felt myself back in my soft, dark world of painless shadows.

How long this twilight existence went on, I do not know. I had only a hazy notion of surfacing for a short time, being cared for, then falling into darkness again. Sometimes I was conscious of voices around my bed, but it was too much effort to open my eyes to see who was speaking.

Then one morning I awakened, and for the first time, took stock of my surroundings. I was in a small room, which I remembered visiting and cleaning, in what seemed a former existence. I remembered other patients occupying the bed. Always they had been those who were dangerously ill, and many had died here. Had I been so very near death? I wondered.

A nurse came in, her uniform rustling importantly. "Good morning," she said breezily. "This is a change. We thought you were doing a Rip-Van-Winkle on us."

I did not know what she meant, but tried to smile. Later on, Dr. Jaeggi came in to examine me, and beamed at the improvement.

"Fine," he said rubbing his hands. "Now we can really feel we are getting somewhere. Plenty of rest and food to build you up is what you need now. Every day you will grow a little stronger, but we won't hurry you."

Another spell of time followed, when I wakened for longer periods, and Dr. Jaeggi made me move my hands, arms, head, and legs; the slightest movement required a supreme effort. Evidently I had never spoken, and this bothered them. I would try to move my head, or hand, or smile in answer to their questions, but no words came when I tried to speak.

Then as I began to have longer periods of wakefulness, fragments of memory gradually began to return. One day I held up my hand, which had grown very thin, and looked at my long white fingers. Something was wrong. What was it? What was missing?

Then I remembered that I had worn a wedding ring on my third finger, and with that thought the past came tumbling back into my mind. Pierre had put that ring on my finger, and I had vowed never to take it off. Where was Pierre now?

Suddenly I thought of my baby, and for the first time I cried out, "Jean-Pierre, Jean-Pierre!" My tongue formed the words awkwardly, but my brain rushed ahead.

A nurse hurried in, and took one look at my face, then with firm hands pushed me back on the pillow.

"Take it easy," she said. "No use getting upset. Lie quietly while I call the doctor."

I stared at the door until Dr. Jaeggi hurried in.

"Now young lady, what's all this about?" he asked, holding my hand, his fingers on my pulse.

"My baby?" I gasped.

"He is being cared for in a children's home," he replied. "He is well and happy."

"How long?"

"Well now, let me see. It is three weeks since you came here and gave us such a fright, but you are improving rapidly, so there is nothing to worry about. Nurse, I think Annalisa should have something to make her rest after the shock of returning memory."

Again I felt the prick of a needle, and my whirling brain was stilled; but from that time, every waking moment was torment. How had I come here? What had happened? Where was Jean-Pierre? Was he being cared for properly?

Dr. Jaeggi chided me because I would not rest and let nature do its healing work.

"What is wrong with me?" I demanded one day.

"Complete exhaustion for one thing, delayed shock, and glandular fever, is as near as we can figure," he said honestly. "Dr. Margaret Roos confided your story to me, and that helped me understand a great deal. By the way, I believe she is coming to see you today. She visited you and rang many times when you were unconscious. She seems to think you are a very unusual young woman."

"Thank you," I said, and felt the tears spill onto my cheeks. At least I was not absolutely friendless.

That afternoon, I asked my young nurse to rebraid my long hair, and prop me up a little.

"Feeling better?" she asked cheerfully. "My, but you must be beautiful when you have color in your cheeks and your eyes are sparkling. You know, for a while we wondered if we ought to cut off your hair; it is so thick and heavy; but it is so lovely, we hated to do it."

I smiled weakly. Pierre had loved my hair; I would have been upset for his sake if it were gone. Often he would take out the pins, undo the braids, and let the heavy ripples fall about my shoulders. Then he would bury his face in it, and tell me how lovely I was.

I knew that I would never feel again the thrill of his touch and the glow of his love, but these memories were comforting. We had been given such a short time of happiness, but it had been so perfect. How glad I was now that I had been able to love him and care for him before the miserable end came. And I still had part of him left to me. Jean-Pierre was his legacy. Always Pierre would be with me, as long as I had our child.

That afternoon, Dr. Margaret arrived, her arms full of parcels.

"Annalisa, how much better you look," she said, bending to kiss my brow. "You gave us such a fright."

"How good of you to worry so about me," I said, my voice husky with tears.

"Nature has a wonderful way of treating our bodies,"

she said briskly, as she sat down. "You needed a complete rest, so you were oblivious to everything for two weeks."

"I didn't remember anything at first," I said. "Then I remembered about Pierre and my little Jean-Pierre. Where is he? Who is caring for him? If only I could see him."

She smiled widely. "I brought him with me, so that you can satisfy yourself about him. Shall I bring him in? The nurses have fallen in love with him."

I could not speak, but evidently the longing in my eyes spoke for me, for she hurried out, and a few moments later came back, leading Jean-Pierre by the hand. He hesitated, stared at me with his big brown eyes, which were so like his father's, then I held out my arms, and suddenly he ran to me, crying, "Mamma, Mamma," and Dr. Margaret lifted him onto my bed.

"Darling, how big you are growing," I said, burying my face in his neck.

"It tickles," he said with a gurgle, and took hold of my braids. "Horsie," he said, holding them in both hands and jumping up and down.

"Not so rough, young man," Dr. Margaret said, and lifted him down. "He is being cared for in a children's home which is run by friends of mine."

"But what about money?" I asked. "How can I pay for being in the hospital and pay for Jean-Pierre too?"

"There will be nothing to pay," was the amazing response. "The Sutters are caring for Jean-Pierre for my sake, because once I saved their child. As for your expenses, Dr. Demmer is helping, as he feels partly responsible for your collapse. He confesses he didn't realize how his wife had treated you. He was under the impression that there was at least another helper in the house. He had never been told that the daily women they used to employ had left because they could not put up with the conditions. His wife has had a stormy passage since you were taken ill. They were afraid at first that you were going to die, then inquiries might have been unpleasant."

Dr. Margaret handed Jean-Pierre a picture book, and he stood by the bedside, his beautifully-shaped black head bent over it.

"Bang-bang," he said, pointing to a gun.

"Poor children, they see and hear far too much of that," Dr. Margaret said. "How much we have to be thankful for, that at least the actual fighting is not on our land, though many are being killed needlessly nevertheless. Do you still read your Bible and pray, Annalisa?" she asked gently.

I could not meet her eyes. She had been so good to me, and I knew that she was one who lived her faith and did not just talk about it.

"I can't reconcile God's love with war and suffering," I said bitterly. "I have tried to understand, but if God really loved the world, He would surely stop all war and evil."

"Then He would have to take away from man all idea of free choice," she replied. "War is caused by man's greed and lust. No man can live to himself. Unfortunately, the evil which man does affects others, so war causes misery and suffering to untold millions of people who long to live in peace; but that does not mean that we too should be evil. Jesus suffered on Calvary to bring peace into men's hearts, no matter what the outer circumstances might be. It's that inner peace which is worth more than anything on earth. How I have prayed that you might find it. Someday, I believe, those prayers will be answered. Now we must go; we have tired you enough."

"But what will happen to Jean-Pierre and me when I leave here?" I asked. "I cannot return to the Demmers."

"No, you will not go back there. We'll find something else."

"Why are you so good to me?" I asked, my eyes again full of tears.

"You know that answer, Annalisa. Christ gave up His life for you, and I love you for His sake. Come, Jean-Pierre, your mamma must sleep now."

He looked at me mournfully, then clung to me.

"I will come to you soon, my darling," I said as brightly as I could. "Be very good for Madame Sutter. Now go with Dr. Margaret."

Obediently he turned, but I could see his lips quiver, and I turned my face quickly into the pillow. Then for a time, I covered my face with the bedclothes and sobbed unrestrainedly; but when at last I managed to regain control of myself, I felt that those tears had somehow cleansed me of much of my bitterness.

Jean-Pierre was well, Dr. Margaret was my friend, and others had shown kindness to me in a way I had never expected. God had taken care of me in my extreme need, and humbly I thanked Him for it, and dared to pray that He would show me the next step I had to take. Now, of course, I know that the Holy Spirit leads only those who belong to Him. Therefore, I really had no reason to blame God for the events that followed.

Next day, I was moved from my quiet room into a busy ward, and began staying out of bed a little longer each day. I could move around, talk to, and help the other patients. I knew that very soon I would have to leave this haven and take up my burdens once more, and although I dreaded that moment, I longed intensely for Jean-Pierre. I had been away from him for so long, that I was afraid he would forget me; and he was all I had left.

One morning, I was handed two letters, which was unusual, for beyond Dr. Margaret, I had no one to write to me. One was from the lawyer, saying that he was going to visit me that afternoon, as he had obtained permission from the hospital authoritiés; and the other was from Uncle Ernst.

My letter had taken some weeks to reach him, but now they wanted me to bring my baby with me and come to live with them. He was sorry he could not send money for my fare, as things were difficult in Italy, owing to the war; but if I could come to Como, I would be able to have a home with them; and Aunt Rita would take care of Jean-Pierre while I was at work. I would be like another daughter to them. They had such a big fam-

ily that two more would make very little difference, and
Uncle Ernst would love me for my mother's sake.

Was this the answer to my problem? I asked myself
excitedly. Could I go to Italy and start a fresh life? Uncle Ernst and Aunt Rita were my only relatives, and at
least this would be a home for Jean-Pierre.

In the afternoon, I was called to a small side room to
see Monsieur Shaffner.

"I was sorry to hear you had been so ill," he began.

"I am almost well now," I replied.

"I have received a reply from Lady Mary's lawyer,"
he said, taking a letter from his briefcase. "As I expected, the estate which had belonged to Lady Mary's father
was entailed, so it went to the nearest male heir. Lady
Mary had a will, leaving what money she possessed to
her daughter. She made no provision for her stepson."

I stared at him blankly. "I didn't know Pierre had a
stepsister. He never mentioned her."

"Perhaps he didn't know. There is evidently some
mystery about it. The daughter was brought up by an
aunt, and did not know Lady Mary was her mother. It
seems that Lady Mary and her first husband parted almost immediately after their marriage, and Lady Mary's
sister adopted the child as her own. Lady Mary continued using her own name after Pierre's father died."

"So there is nothing left for Pierre's child?" I asked.

"I am afraid not. Only a small amount paid into his
account, which is in my charge, and which I feel belongs
to you."

"But your fee?" I questioned. "I must pay you for
your trouble on my behalf."

"What I have done is very little. I wish I could have
brought you better news. Have you any idea what you
will do now?"

"I have heard from my mother's brother who lives
near Como in Italy," I replied. "He has invited me to
take my child and make my home with them."

"And you wish to do this?"

"I don't know, but at least it would be a home for
Jean-Pierre; and I have nowhere else to go. It would be

a chance for me to have a fresh start where no one knows me."

"What do you know of your uncle's family?"

"Very little. I remember that he and his wife came with two small children to visit my mother when I was very young. We haven't kept in touch since my mother died. I know that he and his wife have a large family—about eight children I think—but, of course, some of them will be grown up. He has offered me a home, but I have to find the railway fare myself."

"The money I mentioned will cover that, and leave a little over," he said. "But think carefully before you take such a big step. Remember you will be among strangers in a foreign country."

We shook hands, and I promised to let Monsieur Shaffner know my decision. To me it seemed that the way ahead was clear. We had been offered a home, and now the money was available to pay my fare and buy the extra clothes we would need.

I wrote to Dr. Margaret, telling her of my uncle's offer; and like Monsieur Shaffner, she begged me to think carefully before making such a big decision, but my mind was already made up.

I asked Monsieur Shaffner to purchase our tickets and apply for my visa to Italy. Madame Sutter visited me with Jean-Pierre one afternoon; and when I told her of my decision, she invited me to stay at the home until I was strong enough to travel and had purchased all we needed.

The days passed, and as I grew stronger, a measure of peace returned. Before me was the opportunity to start a new life with Jean-Pierre. Away from Switzerland, I would not be constantly reminded of Pierre and all I had lost. I would be far away from my uncle, who was again demanding that I return to his house. He had no authority over me now, but I was still afraid of him.

My greatest grief was that I would be so far away from Dr. Roos, but she had volunteered for International Red Cross work, so she would not be near Berne anyway, and I promised that I would keep in touch with her. I would never forget all she had done for me, and I would pray every night for her safety. I longed that I would grow to be like her. To me, she was an example of what a Christian should be, but I felt I would never be good enough to reach her standard. It did not occur to me that the same divine grace that made her the person she was, could be mine also.

# 5

Two WEEKS AFTER my discharge from the hospital, Jean-Pierre and I left Switzerland, where I had been so happy but also so unhappy, and set out for our new life.

Jean-Pierre was too young to understand what was happening. There was the great excitement of a train journey, and I was with him; so as far as he was concerned, all was well with his little world.

All through Switzerland, it rained continually. Hour after hour, the windows streamed with water outside, and steamed up inside. I longed to see the beauties of the mountain passes through which we traveled; but with every mile, a greater sense of depression descended upon me. Jean-Pierre grew restless, fell asleep, wakened, was fretful, and slept again. My head throbbed with the uneven motion and the noise of grinding brakes, but I could not sleep. Then as we crossed into Italy, the rain ceased, and the sun shone brilliantly; and as we ran alongside Lake Como, the setting sun threw her last rays on the water. It was as if this were an omen for me. Behind me were months of sorrow, but here was brightness and hope.

I felt bedraggled and filthy, as the train neared my destination, and did my best to tidy Jean-Pierre and myself, but I longed for a hot bath and fresh clothes.

Uncle Ernst and Aunt Rita were waiting at Chiasso station, but they bore no resemblance to the couple in my memory. Uncle Ernst was an old man now; yet surely he could not be so very old in actual years. His hair was white, his body scrawny and bowed at the shoulders, but his eyes in his lined face were kind.

Aunt Rita was fat and dumpy, her skin swarthy, and her gray hair wispy about her florid face. Her dark eyes looked us over almost hostilely, then she started to chatter rapidly; though of course, I could only understand a word now and then. I was soon to learn that Aunt Rita only stopped talking when she was asleep, while Uncle Ernst said very little. Now he translated some of the things she said into French, but I knew there was much he left unsaid.

She made a great fuss of Jean-Pierre, but became offended because he would not leave me to go to her.

"He's very tired," I explained, while Uncle Ernst translated. "Everything is so new and strange, but he will soon settle down. Life hasn't been easy for him these last few months."

When I entered my uncle's house, my high hopes fell with a crash. This was not the sort of place I had expected. After the sparkling cleanliness of Swiss homes, even poor ones, I was appalled at the disorder and poverty.

It was a big old house with patches of green moss growing on the walls and roof. The paint had long disappeared from doors and window frames, and the inside was even worse. The walls had paper peeling off and great patches of damp showing, and what furniture there was, was worn out and of the poorest quality.

The family consisted of seven daughters, ranging from twenty-four down to eight. Giovanni, the only son, whom I remembered from their visit, was in the army; Lucia and Guilia, the two eldest daughters were married, and as their husbands were also in the army, still lived at home. Lucia had two children; and Giulia had one, with another not far off. This meant that altogether there were fourteen of us living in the house; there would soon be another, and when the menfolk returned, that would make eighteen.

It soon became apparent that only Uncle Ernst had wanted me to join this already overflowing household. I could not understand what Aunt Rita and the girls were saying, but their looks and actions were plain enough.

Uncle Ernst was kind, and I was grateful that I could talk to him in French; but the contrast between this place and my former life was staggering. I had never been used to the careless habits of the whole family, or the utter lack of privacy.

Jean-Pierre and I had to share a bedroom with two of the younger children. I had a small, lumpy trundle bed, and Jean-Pierre had an old cot, tied up with string, and a horribly stained mattress, pushed in the corner beside my bed. There was only one small window, and the children complained loudly if it was opened. Soiled clothes were thrown everywhere, and the atmosphere was rank and unpleasant.

For days, I could scarcely believe that people could live in such a fashion. I remembered how particular my mother had been, and was amazed that Uncle Ernst could have become accustomed to such conditions; but I realized even on that first day, that he was of very little account. Aunt Rita and her daughters ruled the roost. Uncle Ernst worked hard; and every penny he earned, he handed over to his wife.

Neighbors came in to stare at me and to discuss me in Italian. My head buzzed with their continuous, high-pitched, excited garble. They fingered my clothes, pointed to my hair, and sneered at my struggle to keep Jean-Pierre even decently clean. The other girls tried on my hats and shoes, wore my dresses without asking permission, and seemed to think they had a perfect right to poke among my possessions.

How often when the others were asleep, I lay awake long into the night, staring hopelessly into the future.

Why had I decided to come to this awful place? I had
thought it was the answer to my desperate prayer; everything had fitted in so well; but if my circumstances were
bad in Berne, they were far worse here.

In my heart, I blamed God. I had prayed that He
would show me the way. I had believed that it was His
plan for me, when I received Uncle Ernst's invitation. If
He had really cared about me, He would never have let
me take this wrong step. And now I had no money to
pay my fare back to the clean sanity of Switzerland. I
was here in a country of strangers, listening to a language I could not understand; and my cup of misery ran
over.

Uncle Ernst had suggested before I came, that I
should find a job; but I could not bear the thought of
leaving Jean-Pierre to the tender mercies of my aunt
and cousins all day; and besides, I could not understand
what people said; so how could I work for them? The
first thing I had to do was to learn the language, and I
set about doing this immediately. As I helped with the
endless cooking and washing, I learned the names of the
things we used, and tried to imitate what was said to me.
No one else made any effort at keeping the place properly clean; so for my own sake and Jean-Pierre's, I
swept the floors, cleaned the windows, and scrubbed the
table, while Aunt Rita and the others shrugged their
shoulders and laughed, touching their heads to suggest
that there must be something wrong with my mentality.

Uncle Ernst was the only one who showed any real
kindness, and from him I could learn more than from
the others. I could ask him words in French, and he
would patiently correct my pronunciation in Italian.

I explained to him that I must learn quickly so that I
could work, but he told me there was no hurry. I was
working hard enough in the house as it was, and my little one needed me. Lucia and Guilia had small army al-
lotments from their husbands; Aunt Rita drew an allowance for Giovanni, the eldest son; Dora, the third
daughter, worked in a wineshop in the evenings; and
Rita, the fourth sister, worked in a factory. The other

girls were still at school. Uncle Ernst declared that he could easily afford to keep me. Jean-Pierre and I ate very little, and besides, I was his sister's child.

He told me once that when he first came to Italy he had longed to be back in Switzerland. Then he had met Rita and fallen in love with her dark beauty and vivacious manner, and they had married. Rita had refused to leave her family and friends; and as their children followed fast upon each other, he had given up all ideas of ever leaving Italy. "I know the house is not kept as Swiss homes are kept, but it is useless to argue and fuss. Everyone else lives in the same way. Rita is just like her neighbors, and is happy and easygoing, as long as nothing upsets her."

"She did not want you to invite Jean-Pierre and me here, did she Uncle Ernst?" I asked him. "It would have been better if we had not come."

"This is my house," Uncle Ernst said, drawing himself up with a pathetic effort at dignity. "You are my sister's child. Of course Rita knew that we did right in having you here to become part of our family. You'll learn to settle down to our ways in time, Annalisa. The Italians are goodhearted for the most part, even if not so organized or hardworking as the Swiss."

Poor Uncle Ernst. He tried so hard to be loyal, and I suppose after all these years, he had become inured to his environment and had learned to live with it; but I knew I would never accept such conditions for Jean-Pierre.

When I had been in Como about two months, word arrived that Giovanni, the son of the house, was coming home on leave. It seemed that with this news, the whole family changed. Aunt Rita and the girls tidied themselves up and even encouraged me to clean more thoroughly. It was obvious that Giovanni was a very important member of the household.

From the moment he entered the house, the atmosphere altered. He was a tall, handsome, young man, very like the mental picture I had of Uncle Ernst years ago. He had his mother's dark hair, but his father's blue eyes and tall figure. Army training had given him a surface superiority, at least. In his uniform, he was a very attractive man, and his mother and sisters obviously adored him. Meals were more regular and better served, for Giovanni had become used to army discipline, and had plenty to say if things were not to his liking.

He was the liveliest sort of person I had ever met, always full of fun and jokes, and kept everyone in fits of laughter. I had learned enough Italian by now that I could join in occasionally; and as Giovanni had learned a smattering of French, he often explained things to me which I did not understand.

From the first day he took a liking to Jean-Pierre and made a great fuss over him; and in return, Jean-Pierre trotted after him as a worshiping shadow. Probably it was this which first attracted me to Giovanni; also there was enough resemblance to my mother and Uncle Ernst to make me feel more at home with him than with the rest of the family, who were so like Aunt Rita. And Giovanni went out of his way to be kind to me. He noticed very quickly that I was expected to do more than my fair share of the work, and he soon had his sisters hopping around far more actively than usual.

Giovanni was obviously popular in the town also. There was a continual round of parties for him. Once or twice he asked me to accompany him and some of his sisters; but I always refused, saying I did not want to leave Jean-Pierre, and I was too tired at night anyway.

I would hear Giovanni and the others returning very late, obviously merry after their night out; but this was natural, I supposed. After all, he was a returning soldier, he deserved all the fun he could have; and drinking wine in Italy seemed as natural as water in Switzerland.

Two days before Giovanni was due to return, he invited me to accompany him for a day on the lake. We would take Jean-Pierre with us, and eat at a cafe where the steamer stopped.

I was sure Aunt Rita and the girls were displeased at the invitation, but they dared not say anything. Uncle Ernst and Giovanni insisted that I needed a break from the continual cooking and cleaning; so at length I agreed, and I was surprised at the mounting excitement I felt as we set off.

It was a beautiful day of bright sunshine and a pleasant breeze, and Jean-Pierre was beside himself with happiness. Giovanni made a wonderful companion; and for the first time for many many months, I experienced the sense of being cared for and treated as someone very special.

As I relaxed on the boat, letting the peace and beauty sink into my starved soul, my spirits lifted. A sense of being young again filled me. After all, I was only twenty-three; how good it was to feel my cares roll away, if only for a few hours. Giovanni appeared to me to be amazingly sensitive. He could join with me in my appreciation of nature; yet at times he could be lighthearted and make me laugh. It felt like centuries since I had laughed naturally, and the years seemed to fall away. Jean-Pierre was a bond between us, and I marveled at the understanding Giovanni showed to him. This was certainly the happiest day I had had since Pierre was taken away from me; but on our return journey, I was brought back to my problems with a great jolt.

Jean-Pierre was asleep in Giovanni's arms, and I sat quietly, relaxed and happy after such an enjoyable day. Then Giovanni began to talk very softly, and I had to strain to hear him over the noise of the engine and swish of the water.

"Annalisa, you hate living with my family, don't you?" he asked. I hardly knew how to reply, so I did not speak.

"I know it isn't what you're used to. Papa has told me your story, and I feel sorry for you, but you can't go on living in such a way. My mother has never been used to anything else, but I have learned to live differently."

Giovanni spoke in a mixture of French and Italian, so that I managed to understand what he was saying.

"But what can I do?" I returned. "I have no money, and I will not part with Jean-Pierre."

"Marry me," he said, and I moved away from him.

He was my cousin, and I had not thought of him as anything else.

"I love you," he said. "And I love Jean-Pierre. I will
take him as my own son. When I'm discharged from the
army, we'll move away from Como to some place where
no one knows us, and start a new life. I'm a good work-
man. With my army gratuity, I'll buy a workshop and a
house; and you will not have to live as you do now. Say
yes, my beautiful darling, and I will apply for special
leave so that we can be married; then you will have my
army allotment until I am discharged."

I had struggled to understand what he said, and my
heart hammered painfully. I liked him, but I did not
love him. I knew I would never love anyone as I had
loved Pierre, but did this mean that I could not marry
someone else and make him a good wife? Then I
thought of how little I really knew of this cousin, and
how unpleasant I found the rest of his family. If I married him, I would have to accept an even closer relationship with them.

"I like you, but I do not love you," I managed to
stammer. "I loved Jean-Pierre's father so much that no
one else can ever take his place."

Giovanni put his free arm around me. "I don't ask
you to do that, my beloved. I'll take such care of you
and Jean-Pierre that you will grow to love me. You are
far too beautiful to let this tragedy ruin your whole life.
You need someone to care for you, provide for you.
Please let me be that one."

"I must think; give me time," I begged. "I cannot decide so hurriedly."

"But I leave in two days," he pressed. "Let's get engaged, then on my next leave we will be married. If
mother and the girls know you belong to me, they'll
treat you differently."

"I will give you your answer tomorrow," I said, and
pulled away from his arm.

"But we can be engaged? Don't send me away without any hope. I may be killed, Annalisa, but at least you
can send me back with the prospect of future happiness

before me. I have never loved another girl like this. I have never wanted to be married and tied down. Now all my heart desires is to have you for my wife, and your child for my son. He is a beautiful boy, sweetheart, and if we live in another town, no one will know he's not mine. With his dark hair and eyes, he could pass as Italian very easily."

I suddenly realized that my hands were aching, and I looked down to see my knuckles gleaming white where I had clenched them in my perplexity.

"I don't want to stay in Italy," I said at last. "As soon as I can save the money, I'm going back to Switzerland. I don't belong here, and I don't fit into the way of life."

"Then we'll go to Switzerland together. I can do my work and make a good living there just as easily as in Italy."

"Would you leave your family?"

"You and Jean-Pierre and the other children we will have, will be my family," he replied simply. "Promise me, sweetheart. You are so beautiful, every man will want you. I can't leave you for someone else to take from me."

"Not even for the sake of Jean-Pierre will I marry a man I do not like and respect," I said trying to speak firmly.

"But you have said you do like me," Giovanni persisted. "I will do whatever you wish me to. Sometimes I drink too much, but that is only because I'm lonely. With you I would have everything to satisfy me. You are better educated, used to a better life than I am, but you could teach me. Help me to rise to better things, beloved."

"I will give you your answer tomorrow," I said. "Please don't rush me anymore tonight. It has been such a wonderful day."

"There will be a lifetime of such days," he promised extravagantly, and I smiled as at a child. I felt so much older and more mature. I knew so well that life is never a succession of peaceful days. There will always be trials and disappointments. A day like this is only an oasis in life. At that moment, I felt almost as maternal to Giovanni as I felt to Jean-Pierre. He seemed like a little boy who needed loving and comforting.

With an obvious effort, Govanni let the subject drop, and exerted himself to be lighthearted again, but as we approached the house I hated so much, he said in a low voice, "I must get you out of this, my beautiful one. Tomorrow, you will say yes. You have nothing to lose, and everything to gain."

As I tossed on my lumpy, uncomfortable mattress that night, those words kept ringing in my ears. "You have nothing to lose, and everything to gain." Certainly the first part of the statement was true, but what about the last? I did like Giovanni and he was so good to Jean-Pierre. Uncle Ernst had told me that before going into the army he had been a clever woodworker and had had a good salary, compared with most Italians. He could earn his living anywhere, and someday hoped to have a workshop where he would employ several men. And Giovanni had promised he would take us back to Switzerland. This was like a dream. Surely away from the influence of his family, we could build a good life together. This seemed such a wonderful answer to my problems.

Then I remembered that before I came to Italy, I had thought the same thing; but what a mistake I had made. I was miserable now, but someday I would be able to leave this hated place. If I married Giovanni, I would never be able to leave; I would be tied to him for better or for worse. This was far too serious a step to decide so hurriedly. I longed for someone with whom to discuss it. If only I could see Dr. Margaret and confide in her. Then I remembered again that in spite of her warnings, and those of Monsieur Shaffner, I had chosen my own way; so I would probably do the same anyway. And it was useless to pray about it, as Dr. Margaret suggested. I had thought God meant for me to accept Uncle Ernst's offer, but look where it had landed me. I would get along without His help; because it was my life after all, and I was the one who had to live with my mistakes.

At last, after going over and over the pros and cons, I decided I would refuse to make any promises. I wanted to be free. If I became engaged to Giovanni, I would have to stay here whatever happened, and I was determined that as soon as I knew the language and could get a job, I would move away.

I still had the few pieces of jewelry which my aunt had bequeathed to me. I would try to sell them. Maybe they would not fetch much, especially in this poverty-ridden area; but someday they would help us to escape.

# 6

———◆———

THE NEXT DAY, the whole family seemed to be staring at me expectantly. Had Giovanni told them that he had asked me to marry him? He did not appear until late in the morning, and I wondered if had been celebrating the night before and was sleeping it off. When he finally came in, he looked bright and cheerful and well-groomed. This, together with his love for Jean-Pierre, appealed to me. He was such a contrast to his surroundings and the rest of his family.

"I have some shopping to do," he announced as he finished his late breakfast. "Come with me, Annalisa, I will help you with your marketing."

"Me too," Jean-Pierre demanded, grabbing Giovanni's hand.

OK. We'll push the baby carriage and look like an old married couple."

I flushed at the sly looks Lucia and Giulia exchanged with their mother, and bent to wipe Jean-Pierre's grubby hands and face. It seemed impossible to keep him clean in this house.

I really did not want to make such an obvious outing, but I had to speak to Giovanni in private.

"Now tell me the good news, and let me breathe again," he said, as soon as we got away from the house.

I clutched the handles of the baby carriage for support, then looking him in the eyes, said as firmly as I could, "I cannot marry you, Giovanni. Please do not argue anymore. I must get away from here as soon as I can, and if I promise to be engaged, I'll have to stay until you come home."

His eyes fell, and for a moment I thought he was going to fly into a rage; then he said calmly, "You'll change your mind yet. Promise you will write to me, Annalisa. I'm not giving up. When I come home, we'll move miles away and start again. I love you, you need me, and I don't give up that easily."

I was glad when we were back home again, and I could get away from the strained atmosphere between us, but things were even more unpleasant than usual. Obviously he had told them I had refused to marry him.

They often forgot that now I could understand much of what they said in Italian when they talked about me between themselves. I was in the kitchen making pies for supper, and I could hear Aunt Rita's high-pitched voice going on and on. She always spoke so fast that I had to strain to make out what she said; but usually it was of no importance, so I did not bother. Now, I realized, Uncle Ernst had just come home, and Aunt Rita was repeating the news to him.

As far as I could gather, she was furious. His stuckup niece thought Giovanni was not good enough for her, and who did she think she was anyway? Giovanni was far too soft, offering to father someone else's child, when he could choose from any of the self-respecting Italian girls who were crazy about him. She was sick and tired of me always pretending I was so much better than they were, poking about cleaning and upsetting the place. They had been happy enough before I came; now it wasn't like home anymore. If Uncle Ernst did not get rid of me, she would make it so uncomfortable that I'd have to go. Why should she and the girls have to give up their room and food for such as me and my child, when I paid nothing?

"Your tongue never stops," I heard Uncle Ernst say sharply. "Annalisa works harder than any of you. She would make a good wife for Giovanni and help him to settle down."

"She'll never marry him if I can prevent it," she said shrilly. "I've had to put up with enough from *your* finicky Swiss ways. Giovanni needs a merry Italian girl who will give him fun. Anyway, they will be out of here as soon as he gets back into the army."

I was unable to get away from the strident voice, and my limbs were shaking as I realized how Aunt Rita hated me. Lucia and Giulia joined in; and for a few moments, I could only hear a jumble of furious vituperation; and I knew that it was all directed against me. Poor Uncle Ernst. How miserable I had made things for him.

Then the noise stopped abruptly, and I heard Giovanni's voice say, "What's all this about? I can hear you down the street."

Aunt Rita broke out again, saying much the same thing; but before many words, Giovanni shouted angrily, "Shut your mouth, you silly old hen. If you'd treated Annalisa decently, and made this place fit for her to live in, she wouldn't have been so anxious to get away. She hates your dirt and laziness. She's the girl I'm going to marry, so you'd better watch how you treat her. She'll change her mind yet and realize that she needs me; but believe me, if you make her any more miserable than she is already, you'll never see me back in this place again.

"Why don't you take a lesson from her, and tidy yourselves up, and keep the place clean? Do you think I want to marry anyone who'd have a house like this? Look at Lucia and Giulia. What have their husbands got to come back to? They are too lazy to run homes of their own, so they pig it out here, with their scruffy kids all over the place.

"Annalisa is worth all of you put together, and don't you forget it. Next time I come home we'll be married, and woe to you if you haven't treated her properly. To begin with, you'll give her a room of her own. Clear out one of the attics, and put some of the kids up there. If you don't do that, I'll stop your money, Mamma, and have it paid to Annalisa."

I could hear Aunt Rita sobbing violently, and Lucia and Giulia yelling at him in rapid Italian.

Then he spoke again. "Papa, Annalisa is your responsibility. You will see that she has the room and has less work to do. It's time you made these lazy women of yours shape up. You're far too soft with them."

"Very well, my son," Uncle Ernst said, a new note in his voice. "It will make me very happy to see you married to a fine girl like Annalisa."

"Where is she?" Giovanni demanded, but no one answered, and I heard steps approaching the kitchen. I dropped the dishcloth I had been squeezing in my hand, slipped through the cellar door, and crouched down on the worn stone steps.

I could hear Giovanni open the back door, then come back and look in the big cupboards. Did he somehow guess that I had been there all the time?

Then he pulled open the cellar door and peered down.

"I thought as much," he said, reaching for my hand, and pulling me up, held me close.

"How did you know I was there?" I gasped.

"I could smell the soap and powder you use. No one else smells so lovely as you. Did you hear all that cackling going on in there?"

"I'm sorry, I could not get away. They would have seen me passing the window if I had gone out the back door."

"Well, now you know that I mean what I say, and Mamma and the girls know it too. First, you are going to have your own room; and if anyone makes trouble,

you are to write to me about it and tell Papa. Mamma
will be more careful after this. Now, give me one kiss to
remember, Anna. That isn't much, when you may never
see me again."

At that moment my heart was filled with gratitude,
and my admiration of Giovanni had grown by leaps and
bounds. Here, surely, was a man who was able to protect me and fight my battles. He had been willing to take
my side against the rest of his family, so why could I not
trust him?

Suddenly my mind was made up. I would send him
away with a measure of happiness, anyway. I would be
engaged to him, and with his ring on my finger, I would
have protection from his family and from other men.

He bent to kiss me on the lips, and I was surprised at
his gentleness. I had expected passion; instead, it
seemed almost like reverence.

I looked at him as he raised his head, and said softly,
"I'll be engaged to you if you still want me, Giovanni."

He stood as if unable to believe his ears; then he took
me in his arms, and kissed me with all a lover's fervor.
He kept an arm around me, dragging me into the living
room, where a muttering, angry scene was still going on.

"Annalisa and I are engaged," he said excitedly.
"You can get ready for a party tonight. Go out and buy
the drinks, Papa," and he threw some bills on the table.
"Invite whoever you like; this will be some celebration.
Get your prettiest clothes on, all of you; and get the
kids off to bed early."

"Please don't have too much liquor," I begged. "I
hate seeing people stupid with drink."

"There will be such a crowd, there won't be enough
to go around for us to get sozzled," he replied, still holding me close. "Gosh, how I'm dying to see everybody's
faces when they see the wonderful girl I'm getting for
myself."

In a miraculously short time, Aunt Rita and the family were dressed and in high spirits, the ill-feeling and
quarreling forgotten, as they rushed here and there telling the news, inviting people to come in to celebrate,

pushing the furniture about, borrowing glasses, bundling
the little ones into bed, and so on. These volatile people,
with their quickly changing moods, never ceased to
amaze me. They could change from tears to laughter,
anger to kindness, hatred to affection in a matter of moments. How different from the more stolid, slow-think-
ing people to whom I was accustomed.

That was an evening I hate to remember. Dozens
and dozens of people crowded in, all shouting and gesticulating at once. Many brought extra bottles of liquor,
and the drink flowed unceasingly. My hand was shaken
over and over again, people shouted at me many things
I could not understand, and both men and women tried
to embrace me continually. My head ached, and a fixed
smile was on my face until my jaws cracked. I had a
glass in my hand, but I never drank from it; and as the
evening went on, I grew more and more disgusted with
the behavior. Men became stupid and stumbled about;
women became uninhibited and clung to any man who
was available. I felt physically sick.

I looked at Giovanni, the man I had promised to marry, and he seemed an absolute stranger. He had had too
much to drink and was in the middle of a crowd of stupid men and women who laughed uproariously at nothing. Suddenly he lurched across to me. "C-come on
sweetheart, join the f-fun," he stuttered and tried to put
his arms around me."

"You're drunk," I said furiously. "I am going to my
room," and slipping away from him, I dashed up the
stairs, pulled the bed across the door, and flung myself
across it, dressed as I was.

This was the first time I had ever been to such a party, although I had been used to people taking a drink
now and again. My father had enjoyed a bottle of wine;
Pierre had taken an occasional drink; I had seen people
drinking in restaurants, but I had never imagined anything like this. I certainly could not marry a man who
regarded this sort of behavior as normal. Tomorrow
morning I would tell Giovanni that the engagement was
off.

The next morning, however, because I had not gone to sleep until the early hours, I slept longer than usual; and when I did go downstairs, it was to find a very subdued household.

Giulia's baby was about to be born. She was already in labor, and I could hear her shrill cries of pain. A strange, untidy-looking woman in a grubby apron was in the kitchen boiling water.

Lucia had banished the younger children to the backyard, and was sitting with Giulia's other child on her lap.

"Giovanni has gone," she said, staring at me with red-rimmed eyes. "He was recalled very early this morning. I guess he was too drunk to know much about it, and he'll wake up to find himself back in camp. That was some party last night, but I gather you did not enjoy it. You've got a lot to learn about men, Annalisa; even if you know more about other things than the rest of us."

I did not reply to this; my mind was in too great a turmoil at the thought that I could not break off the engagement after all.

"Is there anything I can do for Giulia?" I asked.

"Ever helped at a birth?" she demanded.

"I have done quite a lot of nursing," I replied, "and often assisted when babies were born."

Lucia sniffed. "Then maybe you'll be of some use. Mamma is having hysterics, and I can't bear the sight of blood, so old Signora Tonini has to get on with it."

"Will you give Jean-Pierre his breakfast?" I asked.

"It's there, he can help himself," she said, waving to the littered table, where bottles and glasses still remained from the night before. They stood on cupboards and shelves and were piled in heaps in the corners. I lifted Jean-Pierre onto a chair, fed him some milk and bread, then told him to play outside until I called him. I found a clean apron, washed my hands thoroughly, and went upstairs.

Giulia laid on the big bed in her parents' room. Obviously the sheets and pillowcases had not been changed, for they were gray and wrinkled.

The old woman had put pads of newspaper under Giulia, and I shuddered as I thought of what the Swiss health authorities would think. I slipped to my room, took out some clean rags I had washed and bleached in the sun, and returned.

I took cold water and gently sponged Giulia's white, perspiring face and clenched hands, then sponged down her body. She stared at me, and the pitiful entreaty in her eyes wrung my heart. I had been only dimly conscious of the pain when Jean-Pierre was born, but there was nothing to help Giulia or alleviate the birth pangs.

I had learned previously that only as a last resort was a doctor or qualified nurse called in. Giving birth was considered a normal function, painful but necessary, and in a land where children were born to a woman almost every year, nothing to make a fuss about.

The old woman stared at me, then said in Italian, "Are you a nurse?"

I nodded. I thought I could claim this, because I probably knew far more about the practical side of nursing than she did. I slipped the clean rags under Giulia, and wiping my hands with some disinfectant I had brought with me, stooped to examine her.

"Not long now," the old woman muttered. "She's very small. She had a bad time with the last one."

Giulia reached for my hands and grasped them in a grip which hurt, but I did not try to take them away. I glanced at the little pocket watch Pierre had given me and which I usually carried in my purse, and timed the spasms of pain. They were coming regularly now, five minutes between the awful pain, then a short respite to rest. The morning wore on, and I could tell Giulia was getting tired. The pains were now at three-minute intervals. The old woman muttered and began to work on Giulia's body, but she still clung to my hands every time a spasm racked her.

"Annalisa, I'm so tired," she whispered. "Am I going to die?"

"It will soon be over," I said. "Push down with every bit of strength you have, when the next pain comes."

Suddenly she writhed and gave a loud shriek, and the birth was over.

The old woman took up the baby, looked at him, then laid him aside and attended to Giulia, who laid with her eyes closed, white and spent.

I picked up the child and folded him in the rags I had brought. He made no movement; then I remembered what I had seen the nurse doing to Jean-Pierre.

Hardly breathing myself, I held the baby up and slapped him until he gave a loud cry, and I gasped in relief. How terrible if Giulia had gone through all that suffering only to lose her baby. Maybe babies did come along too frequently in this Roman Catholic country, but every child was special to its mother.

I turned to see the old woman staring at me. "Holy Mother," she said reverently. "I thought the little one was dead. It was a difficult birth."

Giulia held out her arms. "Thank you, thank you, Annalisa. I will never forget. How did you know what to do?"

"I saw the nurse do it to Jean-Pierre," I said, busying myself with washing the little one; then I helped to clear up the mess and make Giulia comfortable. I slipped my fresh nightdress over her head, put on clean pillowcases, washed her face, brushed her long black hair, and plaited it into braids. She looked very sweet and helpless when I had finished, and we had laid the little one beside her.

Aunt Rita slipped in just as we were finished. "My poppet, is it all over?" she demanded, rushing to the bed. "The blessed Virgin has answered my prayers. I have been to church to pray, and see how she has cared for you. Ah, how she understands what we poor women have to suffer. She who had her holy Son in a stable, with no other there to help."

"Mamma, my baby almost died. It was Annalisa who brought him back to life, and she was so good to me while the pains were bad. She is a wonderful nurse."

Aunt Rita stared at me with her snapping black eyes. "That is indeed true," the old nurse agreed. "Never have I seen anyone better at such a time. She could earn her living as a midwife. I am getting too old for the strain and responsibility. Always there are so many babies, and so often I have to lose my rest at night. I need an assistant. Would you consider taking on such work, Signora? The money is not much, but there are gifts of other things which help."

My heart was beating violently. Here, without my seeking, was something I could do, but did I dare take it on? Suppose I made a mistake, and things went wrong? At least, I knew the importance of keeping things clean, and probably this old woman knew very little about real medicine. Perhaps I could go with her and assist until I learned as much as she knew. If I wrote to Dr. Margaret, she would send me books and give me advice. All the time I would be learning more of the language, and perhaps saving money to help me escape.

For the next few days, I was so busy caring for Giulia and her new baby, that I had little time to think or worry over what had happened. The baby was delicate and refused to suck, and for days it looked as if all the struggle had been in vain. I managed to keep him alive with a tiny eyedropper, and at last he began to feed normally.

From that time on, I had one more friend in the house. Giulia looked upon me as the fount of all wisdom, and was ready to follow everything I suggested. I taught her how to bathe the baby regularly, and the importance of keeping it clean, and no one was allowed to make any remarks about me. Giulia was my ally, and gradually even Aunt Rita and the others were more pleasant.

I had one letter from Giovanni, written in Italian, telling me how sorry he was for what happened. I struggled, with Uncle Ernst's help, to understand what he had written.

Please forgive me. I am so ashamed, but I promise it will never happen again. I keep seeing the look on your face. How disgusting that was for you. We Italians love our celebrations, and a very

little wine makes us merry. You will probably not
hear from me for a long time, because tomorrow
we are moving to the firing line, and many of us
will not come back. Please light candles and pray
for me, and ask Mamma and the others to do the
same. Please continue to write to me, my darling,
even though you do not get a reply. Only the
thought of your lovely face makes me brave
enough to face what is before me. I want to live to
come back to you and Jean-Pierre.

I stared at the words before me when we had struggled through the letter. How could I write now and tell
him that I had changed my mind, because he had made
a fool of himself at our engagement party? He might
even at this moment be going to his death. I could not
have his unhappiness on my conscience. I must wait until he came back.

In the meantime, I found I had little time on my
hands. Signora Tonini called me in on one case after another. Giulia was always willing to watch Jean-Pierre,
and I found a new satisfaction in helping these people.
Of course, Signora Tonini gave me very little out of
what she was paid, but there were gifts of eggs, fruit, a
bottle of wine, a bag of spaghetti, a long loaf of bread,
or some special buns. But perhaps the greatest benefit
was the change in the attitude of my neighbors. As one
after another learned of what I had done for someone's
daughter, or granddaughter, they began to greet me with
respect. Now the men touched their hats, the women
called out in greeting, and, as I could answer in Italian,
I felt much less of an outsider.

Signora Tonini had been forced to call in Dr. Perrini
on a very difficult case, and I met him for the first time.
Evidently he approved of me, for he asked me to visit
his office and offered to use me on his own cases.

"It is almost impossible to find a fully trained nurse
these days," he said in French. "How much training
have you had?"

"Several courses at the Red Cross school, and a year helping in a hospital as ward orderly," I replied.

"I thought so, and I know any training in Switzerland will be thorough. Here in Italy, one is up against continual ignorance and superstition. They have no idea of cleanliness, and believe if a child dies through neglect, it is because God has willed it so."

"I can't speak Italian fluently," I explained. "And I can't be away from my little boy for long."

"But surely in such a house as Signora Müller's, there will be plenty of women to look after him."

"Maybe, but I do not wish him to grow up as my cousin's children are doing."

"Why did you leave your own beautiful country?" he asked.

"My husband died, I had my baby to support, and I had been very ill. My uncle, whom I had not seen since I was a young child, offered me a home. I came, but it has been a great disappointment. Someday I hope to take Jean-Pierre back to our own country again. That's why I wish to save money for our fare."

"Then I will assist you, if I can, and be glad of your help also."

I went away feeling that here was another ray of hope.

Our next door neighbor received a letter from France written by the French girl her son had married. She asked if I could translate it for her, and I did so gladly. The news spread that I could speak French and German, and soon others who had sons in France or Germany, who sent documents to be filled in, or had received letters from their foreign daughters-in-law, asked for my help; and again I felt that I was gaining people's respect. Even Aunt Rita treated me differently.

One day when Uncle Ernst and I were alone, he said with his tired smile, "You are making us all very proud of you, Annalisa. Everyone in the town is beginning to realize how clever you are, and talk about what you can do."

I laughed. "People know so little, that it is easy to help them."

Uncle Ernst sighed. "They are a poor people, and they are content to live as they have always done. I hear even the marshal of the carabinieri [police] asked you to help with foreign documents concerning emigrants."

"Poor man, he was in a terrible state," I replied. "But I am glad that I find it so easy to learn languages."

"You have picked up Italian very quickly."

I nodded. "I can understand it and can make myself understood now, but I must study the grammar more thoroughly. Dr. Perrini has lent me some books which belonged to his daughter."

Again Uncle Ernst sighed. "I wish we could hear something from Giovanni. The news is not good, and there are many casualties."

"But surely we'd hear if anything really serious had happened?"

"Maybe, but sometimes soldiers are taken prisoner, or are killed, and are left where they are when their company has to retreat. I have my heart set on seeing you married to him. There is a lot of good in the boy, but his mother spoiled him because he was the only son. He needs someone like you to make him take his responsibilities seriously."

For a moment I was tempted to tell Uncle Ernst that I had no intention of marrying Giovanni, and that as soon as he came home, I would break the engagement; but he looked so pleased with the idea, that I put off the announcement which I knew was going to hurt him.

A few days after this conversation, a telegram arrived with the news that Giovanni was, "missing, presumed killed," and the whole family indulged in the most terrible orgy of grief with long wailing and prolonged sobbing. I had never seen people release their emotions so completely. Neighbors flocked in to add to the commotion; and long into the night, the sorrowful lament went on.

I was shocked and sorry, but I could not cry unrestrainedly as the rest were doing; so I kept to my room.

Because I was dry-eyed, Aunt Rita regarded me as completely unfeeling; but I had never cried this way even when I heard of Pierre's death.

My own reactions and feelings were very mixed. Of course I was sorry that Giovanni had been killed. He had been such a fine specimen of manhood, with all his life before him. It seemed such a waste of a life. But secretly I had to admit that I was relieved that now the decision was out of my hands concerning marriage. I was glad I had not told him that the engagement was off. At least I could feel I had sent him away with that little bit of happiness. How much worse I would have felt if I had actually broken my promise to him.

# 7

WITH NEWS OF Giovanni's "presumed" death, Uncle Ernst actually aged before our eyes. He had been quiet before; now he scarcely spoke at all. He went out to work with slow, dragging steps, and ate hardly anything. I realized then that all his hopes had been centered on this only son.

Two weeks after the news concerning Giovanni, Uncle Ernst collapsed at work and was carried home. Dr. Perrini was summoned, but even before he arrived, I knew that Uncle Ernst had had a heart attack and was dying.

He did not regain consciousness, but just slipped away, and the terrible wailing broke out again.

I had not grieved for Giovanni as I did for Uncle Ernst, whom I had grown to love. I had realized from

my own experience, how difficult life must have been for
him. Because he had loved an attractive, vivacious, Italian girl, he had endure a lifetime of disappointment.
How the lazy, haphazard existence that his wife and
neighbors considered a natural way of life, must have
grated on him. What a struggle he must have endured
before he had been able to accept the living conditions
of these people, and for the sake of peace, endure a
home so totally in contrast to the one in which he had
been reared. I imagined that in Giovanni, he had seen a
resemblance to himself, both physically and mentally.
Giovanni was handsome, clever at his trade, better educated, and more particular about his habits than most of
his contemporaries.

The husbands of Giulia and Lucia came home
for the funeral, and I met them for the first time
but was not impressed. Carlo was a lighthearted,
easygoing sort of man; but Lucia's husband, Giorgio,
was the type of man I heartily disliked. He was short
and very dark, and would in later years run to fat, and
his manners appalled me. He gobbled his food, burped
with loud satisfaction afterward, flew into a temper at
the slightest provocation, and obviously imagined he was
irresistible to women. I hated the way he looked at me
and pawed me at the slightest excuse. I noticed that
even with the younger girls, he was too free with his em-
braces, and I felt sorry for Lucia and the sort of life that
was before her.

Aunt Rita was the object of much sympathy. All day,
neighbors came in and out, sitting for hours, while the
crying and the eternal chattering went on. For the time
being, our house was the most important one in the
town.

Our parish priest paid several visits, but I wondered
how much comfort he had to give. As far as I could
make out, his prime concern was how much money
would be given to the church. Poor as most of the people were, no one ever thought to refusing the church's
demands. They might have to go without food, or
clothes, or simple necessities in the home, but the dues

the priest demanded must be paid. He impressed on us the importance of continual prayers for the souls of Giovanni and Uncle Ernst.

After the funeral, people came in and out to drink the wine Aunt Rita had provided; and to me, this seemed a strange waste. It had occurred to me already that with no money coming from Uncle Ernst, finances were going to be even more meager. The money wasted on wine and on the trappings of the funeral, would mean doing without necessities for months to come.

I realized, too, that I could not go on living without paying my full share of expenses. But if I handed over all the little I was earning, how could I save toward escaping to a better life for Jean-Pierre?

With the death of Uncle Ernst, the house was even more miserable, and I realized then how much I had looked forward to his coming home each day. He had represented my only link with my past life, and with him I could talk in French about our own dear country or my parents.

I was kept continually busy, and was glad that often I was too tired at night to think or worry about the future. For the time being, I realized I was living in a sort of vacuum. Aunt Rita needed all the help I could give financially. I handed over all the gifts of food, but sometimes I hoarded a little money in secret. Jean-Pierre and I would need clothes and other things, but I could see no hope of saving toward our fare back to Switzerland.

Then three months after Uncle Ernst died, we had an almost greater shock. Word was sent that Giovanni had not been killed. He had been seriously wounded, and had been captured by the enemy. Later, the hospital where he was had been retaken, and he was being sent home.

The news flew through the town like wildfire, and again Aunt Rita sat in state, while a wild frenzy of rejoicing went on

"The blessed Mother has answered your prayers. The holy church has cared for its son and restored him to his family. You must give a suitable thank offering to the church," was the dictate of our parish priest.

Aunt Rita expected me to be wild with rejoicing, and I can say truthfully that I was glad Giovanni had been spared; but once more, my mind was in a state of turmoil. What would this "return from the dead" mean to me?

I was still determined that I would never settle down among these people. Jean-Pierre must have a better life than this. Before long, it would be time for him to go to school, and he must have the sort of education I had had. In Switzerland no child could leave school before the age of fourteen. We had had excellent teachers, and every family had wanted the best education possible for our children. After fourteen, most of us from German Switzerland had been sent to the French Sector to college, where our studies were in French instead of German, and vice versa. In this way, we learned two languages well. We had always been given money to buy our pencils, pens, and the stamps, which we saved for our school outings. We were given responsibilities, which made us feel mature and grown up.

When I came to Italy, I was surprised to find that so many people could hardly read or write. Many had dropped out of school at a very early age, either because they were needed to work and help their families, or because the school was too far away from their homes.

I wanted Jean-Pierre to have the best education possible. I had no money to give him, but at least I would see that his mind was cared for. I could teach him much myself; but as he grew older, he would have to be able to take his place alongside other children with far greater advantages. Now he was learning to speak Italian with the other children, but I spoke to him in French; later, I would teach him German also. At this time, Jean-Pierre was the only reason I had for living.

I wrote to Giovanni as soon as we had his address, telling him little details of home, but no one could call those missives "love letters." I received one or two short notes written for him by other people, but there was very little real news in them. Obviously he had been very ill and was still in great pain.

Then at last came the day when Giovanni was brought home. The whole family and half the town were at the station to meet him, with flags waving, and plans for a fullscale celebration; but one look at him made me wonder what there was to celebrate. He was a crippled, broken man, bearing no resemblance to the strong, fine specimen who had gone away. A hospital orderly traveled with him, and an army ambulance was ordered to meet him at the station. It was a much more subdued group which surrounded Giovanni as he was helped into the house. Aunt Rita and the girls were sobbing bitterly, and even the neighbors' hearty attempts to cheer him up, fell very flat.

Obviously he was exhausted by the journey, and was carried upstairs and put on Aunt Rita's big bed. Downstairs, we went about with worried faces and hushed voices. Was this really the son and brother we remembered? He looked more like a corpse than a living man.

For the next few weeks, everything in the house revolved around Giovanni. Someone was beside him day and night to care for his every need. He lay for hours, just staring at the wall; then spasms of pain would rack him, and it was pathetic to watch him, and to hear him moaning in agony.

We could ill afford it, but Dr. Perrini had to pay constant visits, giving what drugs he could to alleviate the pain, or suggesting ways of helping him.

We learned that a shell had burst beside Giovanni, and dozens of pieces of shrapnel had entered his body. Many of them had been removed, some had developed gangrene, and some were in areas where it was too dangerous to operate.

"Why can't they let me die?" was his continual cry. "Why keep a helpless wreck like me alive? Doctor, give me something to put me out of my misery."

I was naturally expected to be his chief nurse, and when I was there, it was obvious that he was more content. He never slept without a drug, and it was during these spells when I had to snatch what rest I could.

"Signora Müller tells me you are engaged to her son," Dr. Perrini said, looking at me closely one day.

"I promised to marry him the day before he left, but I wanted to break that promise immediately. I realized I did not really know him, and was only accepting his offer because it would mean a home for Jean-Pierre. But how could I tell him this when he was going away to face death? How can I tell him now, in the state he's in?"

"But surely you will never marry him. Do you realize you will have a permanent invalid—if not worse—continually on your hands?"

"But will he get better?"

"I don't know. I don't think he will die, but I doubt if he will ever be strong and normal again."

"Then for the time being, I must go on pretending that all is well between us," I said firmly, though my heart sank.

"Don't let your head rule your heart, Signora. You are one of those who cannot resist suffering, but remember marriage is for a lifetime. Wait until you are perfectly certain what sort of man he has become."

Very, very slowly, Giovanni struggled back to a semblance of life. Sometimes he was pathetically grateful for what was done for him, sometimes fretful and ill-tempered until we were driven to distraction. But we always made excuses: he was suffering so much; and when the pain lessened and he grew stronger, things would be different.

Gradually he began to stumble around his room; then he was helped downstairs, and we fixed up a bed for him in the big living room.

One leg was crippled, and it was obvious he would always walk with a limp, but his arms and hands were healed. His face was marked, and one eye damaged, so that never again would he look like the handsome, happy boy who had made his home such a lively place.

He could not bear to have me out of his sight. I had

to spend practically every waking hour with him. He refused to allow me to take any more maternity cases; and when I mentioned the matter of money, even Aunt Rita declared that they did not want my money. All they wanted was for Giovanni to be happy, and obviously I was the only one who could make him that.

As he grew stronger, there was a rather sweet gentleness about him; and because he depended on me, I found myself thinking of him with almost maternal affection. I have never been able to resist those in pain or suffering, and Giovanni drew out all the resources of patience and sympathy I had.

People regarded him as a hero; to me, he was a little boy who needed a great deal of love and understanding. I saw in him many traces of Uncle Ernst. There was an acceptance of his limitations rather like a dumb animal, and I began to feel that I loved him; not, of course, in the way I had loved Pierre, but at least with some real affection. I know now that this was not the sort of love on which a happy marriage could be built, but I was blinded by the thought that he needed me. For the past three years, I had been tossed about with no permanent anchor, but here was someone who wanted me, and depended on me. Surely what love I had for him would be sufficient, and I would spend my life caring for him and for Jean-Pierre.

For months Giovanni did not mention our engagement, but seemed to take it for granted that I belonged to him. Then one day when he was able to sit out in the garden, he said suddenly, "When are you going to marry me, Annalisa?"

"You're not strong enough to think about that yet, Giovanni."

"I've thought about nothing else for months and months. All the time I was in the hospital, going through such awful pain, all that kept me going was your memory. I had something to live for. If you hadn't been there, I would have let myself die. It was the thought of having you as my wife that gave me the will to live. If you let me down, I'll kill myself, and that won't be difficult with all the sleeping pills I have available. You aren't in love with someone else, are you, Anna?"

"Of course not," I said emphatically.

"Then you won't go back on me?"

"Please leave it until you are stronger."

"No, I have to have my answer now. Marry me, or I'll finish things off. What else have I got to live for?"

"This isn't fair. You're threatening me. If I do marry you, what are we going to live on?"

"There will be my disability pension."

"You promised you would take me back to Switzerland."

"So I will, but not until I'm more like a whole man again. I don't care where we live, as long as we are together." Then stretching out his hand, he clutched mine, saying wildly, "You've got to promise, Annalisa. I've suffered all this to come back to you."

"You'll send your temperature up again," I said gently. "Yes. I'll marry you Giovanni, but not until you don't need me as a nurse."

"You mean, if I'm never able to be like a normal man and do an ordinary job, the deal is off?"

"No, I don't mean that. I mean for the time being you're not fit for all the excitement and strain. As soon as Doctor Perrini says you are fit enough, then I'll marry you."

Suddenly the tears poured down his face, and my heart went out to him. "My darling, I am a poor, broken specimen now, but I'll love you and try to make you happy," he said. "You are so beautiful, you deserve so much better, but no one will ever love you more than I do. My very life depends on you."

"I know," I said, soothing him as I would a child. "But you won't always be like this, Giovanni. Look how much better you are than when you came home. In time, you will be back to normal. I believe we could make a good marriage for ourselves. Both of us have suffered, and are no longer irresponsible children."

At that moment I felt like an old, old woman. I realized that I was putting away any traces which remained of my youth; but I had already gone through so many tragedies, that I believed I could make Giovanni a good wife and build a useful life. Being needed was a very important necessity to me.

I had had my moments of great love, and no one could take those memories from me. But they were only memories now, and I had so many years of life before me. I had met so few men I could trust, that I was continually on the defensive. With Giovanni as my husband, there would be protection for me. I believed that love would never come to me again as I had felt for Pierre. This might be second best, but I would have some sort of happiness.

So I argued with myself that night when I was in my own room. Giovanni would have his pension, and maybe later on would be able to work again. I could take a job if necessary, so at least we would be provided for.

From that day he improved rapidly, and was so kind and affectionate to me and Jean-Pierre, that I felt I had made the right decision; in fact, I began to plan for the day when we could have a home of our own, away from all this crowd and squalor, and live as I wanted my family to live.

Then suddenly one night, Giovanni became violently ill and was in great pain. Dr. Perrini said he must go at once to the military hospital, as he believed an undetected piece of shrapnel was causing the trouble. So Giovanni was rushed away by ambulance, and he insisted that I go with him. For hours I waited, but finally the verdict was an immediate operation; otherwise it was possible that the shell fragment could reach his heart and kill him. The doctors did not mince words when they told me that there was only a slight chance of his surviving the operation.

Giovanni, too, demanded to know what chances he had of recovery, and was told that without an operation he might die at any moment; with the operation there was a fifty-fifty chance. He had never been slow mentally, and he could read more into their words than they actually said.

"It is up to you to decide, but it is necessary to operate immediately."

"I want to get married first," he said, and they looked at him as if he were crazy.

"That's impossible, you must realize that."

"Then I won't have the operation. Anna, tell them you'll marry me as soon as the priest can get here."

"But why?" I asked in bewilderment.

"If we are married, and I die, you will get my war pension."

Nothing would shake him, and as it was so necessary to keep him quiet, a priest who was visiting in the hospital was brought in, and there, around the hospital bed with a doctor and nurse as witness, I became his wife.

For the next three days, Giovanni's life hovered in the balance, and I only left his bedside to rest in a nearby room. Aunt Rita and some of his sisters arrived, but were not allowed to see him. Aunt Rita burst into violent sobbing, as she so often did when she heard of the marriage. Whether it was the loss of the pension she could have claimed, or because she had never wanted me for a daughter-in-law, I was not quite sure; but obviously she felt cheated.

At length, Giovanni was taken off the critical list, and his recovery was rapid.

"It's like a miracle," the doctor who operated on him congratulated him after a final examination. "I have never performed such a tricky operation before. I didn't believe you could recover. Now there's no reason why you should not be a healthy man. The dangerous fragment is removed, and your heart is undamaged. May you have a long and happy life," he said, bowing politely to us both.

I was too tired with the strain and lack of sleep to think straight. Anyway, the die had been cast; I was married to Giovanni now, so there was no looking back.

A week later, when I went to the hospital to visit him one afternoon, he was full of suppressed excitement. I thought it was because he was getting up and moving around again, and was feeling better.

He talked about all sorts of things in our mixture of Italian and French. Then, unable to restrain himself any longer, he said, "I've heard of a house we can live in."

I could scarcely believe my ears, for houses were at a premium.

"Where?" I demanded, my excitement mounting at the first hint of getting away from Aunt Rita's home. Any sort of shack would be like heaven after these months of overcrowding.

"I don't suppose it's much," Giovanni said, reaching for my hand. "Only a room and kitchen, and two bedrooms upstairs. But there is a garden and a big shed, where I can work when I get started again."

"But where is it, and how did you hear of it?" I asked, almost as excited myself as he was.

"Father Pietro visited me yesterday. One of his parishioners has died, and the man's daughter is moving in with her mother, so her house will be vacant."

"Is it near Como?"

"No, it is in Piemente."

"Where is that?"

"A little place about ten miles away. I want you to go and see it, and decide if it is usable; but remember, my darling, this is only to start with; as soon as we can afford it, we will go to your beloved Switzerland."

"Is there a bus to this Piemente?"

"I expect so. Father Pietro gave me the address, and he has told the woman who lives there that you are coming."

"But who owns the house? Is this woman a tenant?"

"Of course. The house belongs to Count Burgano, but Father Pietro has promised to speak to the agent about it."

"But how can we buy furniture and the essentials we must have to start housekeeping?" I asked.

"Ask Signora Brucianni if she has anything she will sell. I have some money saved from my army pay, and we can borrow for what else we must have. Tell me you are pleased, my darling."

"If we can be on our own, it will be wonderful," I

said joyfully. "Just you and me and little Jean-Pierre. I will go early in the morning; then come to tell you about it in the afternoon."

"How beautiful you are when you look happy," he said, pulling me down beside his chair. "Oh, how I love you. How can I wait until you are really and truly mine? I promise you will never regret marrying me, my lovely one. You believe I love you, don't you?"

"Yes, I believe you," I said gently.

"And you love me, I think."

"Yes, I love you," I replied. "I will try to be a good wife to you, Giovanni."

With that, he seemed perfectly content. What I had said was true. I did love him, but there was no glory in it. When he touched me, my bones did not melt, as they had done when Pierre had been near me. The love that had been between Pierre and me had been indescribably wonderful. There had been a beautiful, fragile, intangible bond between us that had no place in this mundane world. Sometimes I told myself it was because we had known it was likely to vanish at any moment, that we had grasped at it and held it to us with trembling hands. Maybe it could not have lasted on such a plane, but it would never have become commonplace. We would never have taken each other for granted.

I was almost glad that my feeling for Giovanni was different. I had no thought that I was giving him what had once belonged to Pierre. Part of me had died when Pierre had been taken from me; what I felt for Giovanni was only a physical emotion. I was willing to care for him, to bear him children, but I knew that there would never be any spiritual involvement between us. I believed that he was incapable of the depth of sensitivity that had been in Pierre, so he would never know that he was being cheated.

The next morning, I borrowed an old bicycle and set off for Piemente. I had told Giulia about the possibility of the house, but asked her to say nothing until I returned, and to take care of Jean-Pierre for me. The others probably thought I was paying an early call to the hospital, but I did not enlighten them.

As I neared the small town of Piemente, the sun was blazing, and I began to wish I had gone by bus after all. I was hot and dusty, so I stopped outside a little cafe to have a drink of lemonade and tidy myself as best I could.

I wheeled my bicycle until I found the address written on the paper Giovanni had given me; then I stood looking at it from the outside. It was certainly nothing imposing. Just an ordinary, shabby little cottage, standing in an untidy garden, with what was obviously the toilet at the side, and in the back a big wooden shed with a dilapidated roof. Nevertheless, I coveted that poor little house with an almost desperate longing. I had never had a house of my own. However poor it was, I could make it clean, and we would be private. I was glad that it stood on its own, instead of in a long row, like so many of the other houses. I saw in my mind's eye what it could look like with a fresh coat of whitewash, window boxes in which red geraniums bloomed, the yard cleaned up, and the roof of the shed mended. With shining windows and clean white curtains, it would be like a little Swiss house.

Nervously I propped up my bicycle, walked along the broken path, and knocked at the door.

A woman of about thirty opened it, a baby in her arms and two more holding her bedraggled skirt.

"You are Signora Brucianni?" I asked in my careful Italian.

"Si, si, what can I do for you?"

"Father Pietro told my husband, who is in the hospital, that you are giving up your home."

She frowned in an effort to understand what I said, then as if the light had suddenly dawned, she said, "Si, si, I go to my mamma. You want to live here?"

"Yes, please," I replied.

"Then please come in. I am packing to go at once, and everything is upset." She dumped the baby in a wicker cot, and waved her arms wide.

"This house belongs to Count Burgano, but I have not told the agent yet that I am leaving. Father Pietro is the only one to know, because he buried my papa and is my mamma's priest."

"Then I must ask Count Burgano if I may have it?"

She shook her dark, untidy, black head. "We have never seen the count. His agent comes to collect our rent. Today is the day. You ask him if you want to live here. Come, and see for yourself."

There was not much to see. The room in which we were talking was a good size, but very dirty and badly furnished; a kitchen with a rusty stove, and a rough, shallow stone sink. Upstairs there were one large and one small bedroom; outside was the bucket toilet, where flies buzzed in a cloud as we approached the door, and the old hut, which was filled with all sorts of odds and ends.

"It is poor," she said, waving her hands. "But we have no money to get a better place. My husband is in the army, and everything is so expensive. It will be cheaper for me to live with my mamma, and she will help me with my little ones."

There was a knock at the door, and a short fat man walked in.

"Good morning, Signora, how hot it is," and he wiped his head with a big spotted handkerchief; then put a book on the table.

"You will have a little wine, Signor Bagatti?"

"Thank you, yes."

Signora Brucciani took out a half-empty bottle and poured a glass of wine for him.

He swallowed it at one gulp.

"Signor, I have to tell you today that I am giving up this house and going to live with my mamma in Como."

"*Accidente!* Then we will have scores of people fighting for it."

"Signora Müller has come to ask if she can have it."

He looked me over from head to foot. "Where do you come from?"

"From near Como," I said carefully.

"Have you a house already?"

"No, we have to live with my mother-in-law. There are fifteen of us living there altogether. My husband has been badly wounded, and will not be able to fight again. We want a home when he comes out of the hospital."

He pulled his long, drooping mustache. "How much can you pay?"

"What does Signora Brucciani pay now?"

"That doesn't count. Rents are going up every time a new tenant comes in. We have to do that to meet the rising costs of repairs and so on."

"I pay fifty lire a month, Signora, but I have had no repairs since we came five years ago," Signora Brucciani broke in.

"The war has stopped all that," he said testily.

"The rain comes in the roof, there is no paint anywhere, the outhouse is broken down," Signora Brucciani cried shrilly, evidently delighted that she could throw discretion to the winds and get all her complaints in at once.

"You're lucky to have such a nice house for so little rent," he said angrily.

"Ask Count Burgano to visit his tenants," Signora Brucciani shouted. "How would he like to live in a place like this? If you put up the rent then you ought to be forced to do the repairs first."

"That is my business," he said angrily. "I have a long waiting list of people who will jump at the chance of such a house and pay twice the rent you are doing."

Signora Brucciani sniffed. "Then it is racketeering, and you know what the government has to say concerning that. What about all the talk of having homes for our fighting men to come back to?"

"Please," I broke in. "My Italian is not good, and I find it hard to understand what this is all about. My husband has been very ill; it is essential that he has a quiet home to come to. We will pay what is fair and do the repairs ourselves."

Signor Bagatti leered at me in the way I so heartily disliked. "What is your nationality?" he asked.

"I am Swiss, but my husband is Italian."

"I would like to help you, Signora, and it is good to help our heroes also. When do you leave, Signora Brucciani?"

"In two days. My mamma cannot bear to live alone for much longer."

"Then you will pay the rent until the end of the month?"

"I suppose so."

"Good, then Signora Müller can take over in three days' time. The rent will be raised by twenty lire, Signora; and I would like twenty lire paid now, as key money, you understand."

"I don't have that amount with me, Signor, but I can have it for you tomorrow."

"Very well, I will be here at the same time. I am delighted to be of service to so charming a lady. How did you know that the house was becoming vacant before I did?"

"Father Pietro visited my husband and told him about it."

"Ah, the church hears all our little secrets. Then I will see you tomorrow, Signora," and he bowed himself out.

"The old Jew!" Signora Brucciani said, making a face as she closed the door. "It's disgraceful to charge so much for such a hovel. And I warn you, Signora Müller, he is very fond of women. I saw the way he looked at you. He hopes you will be an accommodating tenant. There are some women who are not particular."

I made out the gist of what she was implying, and I felt my face flushing. "My husband will be able to deal with him," I replied. "Is there anything you want to sell?" I asked. "We have nothing, and perhaps could buy from you."

She laughed. "What poor things we have are not worth selling. There is the big bed, but one leg is broken. There is no room for it in Mamma's house. This old table and the chairs are worth very little. Ask your husband how much he will give me for them."

"Thank you," I said gratefully. "You are being very kind."

"I am glad someone like you is coming here. It is a miserable place, but it was our home. Our babies were born here, but now I don't need it."

"Then I'll come tomorrow morning to pay Signor Bagatti the money."

"The next day the house will be yours."

She waved as I mounted my bicycle, and as I looked back, that little house appeared as a dream palace to me. Suddenly a home was taking shape, and the future looked bright and hopeful.

Back home I told Aunt Rita and the others that the house was to be Giovanni's and mine in three days' time.

Aunt Rita glared at me; then as usual, burst into a flood of tears. "Then you take my son from me," she screamed. "The only man left to me. Papa has gone; now you take my Giovanni. Always, since the day you came, you have brought bad luck to this house. How happy we were before. Now I have no husband and no son."

"Mamma, that is not true," Giulia broke in.

"Don't you contradict me," her mother snapped. "Will I never have anything but a houseful of squabbling women?"

"But all of us could not have continued to live here," I ventured.

"Lucia and Giulia will go when the war is over. It is right that Giovanni should have been here to care for his mamma and the little ones."

I realized it was useless to argue, so getting Jean-Pierre ready, I set off for the hospital. The sooner we were away from Aunt Rita, the easier life would be for all of us.

Giovanni greeted me as if he had not seen me for weeks.

"We have the house," I said, as soon as he had sobered down.

"What is it like?" he asked.

"Only a poor little place, but we can paint it; and when it is clean, it will be a nice little house, but I am afraid we have to pay quite a lot for it."

"I don't care what we pay, so long as you and I can be there and call it our own. When I'm better, I can work on it."

"Your mother is very angry."

"Why?"

"Because you are not going to live at home. She says now that Uncle Ernst has gone, she ought to have one man left to her."

"Holy Mother, how women rant and rave. Does she want me to be tied to her apron strings forever? I won't be far away if she needs me; but with all that gang around her, she'll never be lonely."

"She doesn't like me, and is mad because you married me," I said. "I wish we were moving further away."

"O, Mamma will get over it. No girl would have pleased her. Because I am the only boy, she never wanted me to grow up. She wanted to keep me a little boy. When the war is over, we'll go to Switzerland, my darling; I promise you. Now tell me what happened."

I described Signora Brucciani, and made the house sound as good as I could, then told of Signor Bagatti's reactions.

"The old skinflint," he said, when he heard of the raised rent and the key money. "I bet Count Burgano knows nothing of it, for it will go into the agent's own pocket. But I guess we're lucky to get any sort of house at all, and we'll make it do until we find something better. Did you ask about furniture?"

"There is very little, and it is poor and broken."

"Then I suppose Signora Brucciani would have to pay more than it is worth to have it moved. Offer her twenty lire for it, if you think it is worth it, sweetheart. Reach in that drawer and give me my wallet."

He took out some notes and handed them to me, saying as he pulled me down to him, "The first money I have given my wonderful wife; and I filled in the forms

for your army pay or pension allowance this morning, so
soon you'll be able to draw that each week."

"Will your mother be able to manage without it?" I
asked.

Giovanni nodded. "Lucia and Giulia pay their share,
Dora and Rita are working, and Juliana leaves school
soon. No matter how much Mamma had, she would always be hard up, because she wastes it on junk. I know
my careful Swiss wife will make money go twice as far."

Next morning, Giulia fixed a sort of carrier on the
back of the borrowed bicycle, and strapping Jean-Pierre
on it, I cycled to Piemente. I found Signora Brucciani
surrounded by bundles and packages, and herself and
the children dressed for traveling.

"A friend of my papa's is coming with his cart to take
us to Como this morning," she explained. "So I'm glad
you came early."

"Will twenty lire be enough for the things you have
left behind?" I asked.

"It is not much," she said grudgingly. "I might have
got more if I had sold the stuff in Como."

"But you don't have to pay for it to be moved," I reminded her.

"I'll take it," she said; and I knew that she was delighted with what I had offered, but it would have been
beneath her dignity to say so.

I knew it was not worth that much; but at least it
would mean Giovanni could come straight here from the
hospital, instead of becoming enmeshed with his mother
again.

Signora Brucciani pointed out all the wonderful things
she was leaving; but most of it would have to be thrown
out anyway, or would need a great deal of repair. What
curtains there were, were dirty and torn; there were several pans with holes in them; a bucket without a handle,
wornout brushes, and so on. The first and foremost need
was plenty of soap, boiling water, and hard work.

Signor Bagatti arrived, but there was no wine for him
this morning. His black eyes gleamed with satisfaction,
however, for Signora Brucciani had already paid him a

full month's rent. I gave him the key money he had demanded, and also a month's rent, starting from that very
morning.

Signora Brucciani explained the vagaries of the old
stove, where the toilet was emptied, how the pump
worked for water, and so on. Then the cart arrived, and
I helped her pile her belongings on it. She climbed up
with the children packed between her and the driver,
and I waved them good-bye. Then I closed the door and
lifted Jean-Pierre in my arms, and danced around the
untidy room with him.

"Mamma, again," he shrieked.

"Jean-Pierre, this is our own little house," I sang.
"You and I are going to make it all clean and beautiful
for when Papa comes home."

I had already decided that Jean-Pierre should call
Giovanni "Papa." If he was to be taken as his own
child, then we must start at once as a real family.

I had told Giovanni that I might not visit him until
the evening, if Signora Brucciani needed help clearing
up; so now I took a big apron from my bag and set to
work.

The stove was lit, and there was plenty of rubbish
lying around to keep it going for many days.

I put the old bucket and every pan which would hold
water, on to heat, and started to pick up the accumula-
tion of odds and ends. Upstairs in a cupboard and in a
sack in the shed, I found huge bundles of discarded
rags. Evidently Signora Brucciani had never bothered to
mend anything. If it was torn, it was thrown away. I
pulled out stained, torn pieces of bed linen and various
garments, and looked at them as if they were gold. I
could easily turn these sheets sides-to-middle, or make
pillowcases out of the small pieces. Some would do for
curtains, which I could embroider Swiss fashion.

There were children's clothes that were stained and
torn, but some of them would fit Jean-Pierre. Things
which had been used by the children were in a filthy
state, but water and hot sun would make them usable. I
felt as if someone had left me a valuable treasure.

Jean-Pierre toddled around with me, picking up pieces of paper and other litter in a little basket. This was a new kind of game for him.

We rummaged in the shed, and I found chairs which had been broken and thrown in there to await repair, an old chest of drawers, a cracked mirror, rusty garden tools, and plenty of wood. What a wonderful time Giovanni and I would have fixing this place up.

I had brought some food with us, so after I had scrubbed the old table and two of the chairs, Jean-Pierre and I had our first meal in our own home, and how good it tasted.

Then I started to sweep the walls, windows, and floors, the dust making us sneeze so much that I ordered Jean-Pierre to play in the untidy yard. He found some broken toys the Brucciani children had left behind, and he pushed them around and around in delight. *Poor little boy,* I thought, watching him from the window. How satisfied he was with so little.

For a moment, my eyes misted. How different his life would have been if Pierre had lived to raise him as his son. Then I shook myself. It was useless to look back. I must put all such memories behind me. I had promised to make Giovanni a good wife, and I would keep that promise, and how much easier it would be, now that we had a place of our own.

That night when I turned the key in the door, I was almost too tired to lift Jean-Pierre onto the carrier, and my legs ached so that I could hardly push the pedals around. I made up my mind that I would move our few belongings to Piemente the next day, after I had visited Giovanni. He would understand that I was getting the house ready for him, and not expect me every day. That would save me this long journey, and I would have time to settle to the real job of cleaning the place thoroughly.

"You look exhausted, Annalisa," Giulia exclaimed, when I staggered in, Jean-Pierre asleep in my arms.

"Signora Brucciani left this morning, so I have started cleaning up," I replied.

Aunt Rita glared at me. "And I suppose no one ever cleaned a house before," she snapped.

I was too tired to reply, but my eyes filled with tears as I stumbled upstairs and laid Jean-Pierre in his cot. How I would have loved a bath, but the best I could do was a basin of lukewarm water. I was determined that somehow we would have a bath of some sort in our little home.

Giulia crept up behind me. "Take no notice of Mamma," she whispered. "She will get over it, and in a little while tell everyone what a wonderful house her precious son has. Get into bed, Anna, and I will bring you some supper."

The only person I was going to be really sorry to leave was Giulia. I almost wished we had room to take her with us. I had never had a sister, and I had come to realize how sweet Giulia was, and how different she could have been in other surroundings.

Gladly I washed off some of the filth and threw myself on the bed.

Guilia brought up a plate of food she had reheated, but I was too tired to eat it. All I wanted was plenty to drink.

She curled up on the end of the bed saying, "Tell me about it, Annalisa."

So I told her about the departure of Signora Brucciani and her family, the mess that was left behind, the old stuff I had found; and she looked at me with round eyes.

"But Anna, think of all the work you'll have. Surely you are not trying to get it all done before Giovanni comes out of the hospital."

I laughed. "It will take months to make it really decent. Giovanni will be able to help when he is stronger; but if it is clean, we can live there and do the rest bit by bit. I'm going to pack our things and go there to live tomorrow."

"Then leave Jean-Pierre with me."

For a moment I was tempted; then I thought of the scant attention he would get anyway, so I said, "It is sweet of you to offer, Giulia. You are like a real sister to me now, and I don't want to leave you, but I want Jean-Pierre to get used to his new home, so that there will be no big change for him when Giovanna comes home."

"I love you better than any of my sisters, Anna," Giulia said, her lovely eyes full of tears. "You have taught me so many things. I'm trying to be like you, but Mamma and the others make fun of me Soon I hope to have a home of my own; but soon, too, there will be another baby. I almost wish Carlo had not come home for Papa's funeral."

"Oh, Giulia, I am sorry," I said gently. "It is so soon after Little Romano."

"That's what comes of being Roman Catholics," she said unexpectedly. "Carlo says other people don't always have babies like we Italians do, but the priests are angry if we try to prevent conception."

I nodded. "It is good to have children of course, but not so quickly that the mother cannot regain her strength."

# 8

IN THE MORNING, I packed our few belongings, cleared the room we had used, then visited Giovanni. He looked so much better, and was talking eagerly about our new home.

I told him I was moving there after I left the hospital, so I would not be able to visit him so frequently. There was so much to do that I would have to spend every moment making the place ready for him to come home.

"But you'll get too tired," he said gently. "We'll have fun doing it together, my darling."

I nodded. "All I hope to do is to get it really clean and fit to live in. I'll have to try to get bed linen and other things we must have, at the secondhand store."

"You'll need more money. Take all I have, sweetheart."

"Keep some for cigarettes or what else you may need," I said, touched at his generosity. "On my way out, I'll ask the doctor or sister when you are likely to be discharged; than I can plan what I have to do."

"I believe you are as excited as I am," he said, pulling me close.

"I've never had a home of my own, and I want it to be as nice as I can possibly make it for you."

"I've been thinking that we ought to have Jean-Pierre's name changed to Müller; then he can really feel he is my son. Would you like that, my darling?"

"Oh, I would," I replied gratefully. This would make things so much easier for Jean-Pierre in the future, if he were legally adopted.

I left Giovanni, with my heart warm and happy. He was being so thoughtful and kind and doing all he could to make our marriage start off well. I would do everything I could to fulfill my side of the bargain.

As soon as we reached our little house, Jean-Pierre and I set off shopping. We had to buy a supply of food; then I found a secondhand store, and very carefully chose only what was absolutely necessary: a pair of blankets, some dishes, pans, and scrubbing brushes. The owner, delighted at selling so much old stuff at once, offered to have it sent around on a handcart when his son came home.

As soon as Jean-Pierre was asleep on the big old bed, I mapped out a campaign. First I lit the stove and put the piles of curtains, old sheets, etc., on to soak, so that I could wash them and put them out on the grass to bleach, early in the morning.

Then I scrubbed out the cupboards, cleaned the windows, and started on the floors. Already the place was beginning to smell much sweeter. The next morning, I was up early. I washed and spread out the linen, blackleaded the stove, which would need days of work before it had a shine on it, then went to the shops and bought paint, brushes, and whitewash.

First I painted the inside window frames, and colored the walls of the living room. Then when the lamp was lit, and it was too dark to paint, I ironed the curtains very carefully and mended the worst of the holes. The next morning, when I hung them up again, they looked fresh and trim, and worth all the effort.

I scrubbed, painted, and colored each room in turn, and by bed time each night, felt almost too tired to crawl upstairs.

I pulled the old cot from the shed, gave it a coat of paint, tied it up as best I could, and put it in the second bedroom for Jean-Pierre.

My neighbors were obviously consumed with curiosity at what was going on; but I asked no one into the house, because I was too busy for idle chatter, and I wanted no entertaining until my house was as clean as I could make it.

I only visited Giovanni once that week, and he objected strongly to the neglect.

"But it is for you I am doing all this," I remonstrated.

"I know, but can't you guess how long the days are, waiting to see if you will come? Anyway, the doctor says in two more weeks I will be home, then I'll have you to myself—every day."

"Two more weeks," I said as I went home in the bus with Jean-Pierre, "and there is still so much to do."

I had made up my mind that I would have the outside of the house whitewashed, at least. Giovanni would not be able to climb ladders, so it was no use waiting for him to do it. I knew that if I did it myself, the Italians would be shocked. This was not the sort of work for a woman. In Switzerland, women had been able to work as hard as the men. They helped in the fields with the cattle, joined in the working of painting and whitewashing, and even building.

I decided to borrow a ladder, and do what I could without scandalizing the neighborhood. I had noticed a builder's yard some streets away, so rather hesitantly, I asked the owner to rent me a ladder for a few days. I had no difficulty making him understand what I wanted; then he was all smiles, and graciously offered to carry the ladder home for me. Obviously he thought my husband wanted to repair the roof or mend a window when he came home on leave.

I got up the next morning as soon as it was light, and painted the window frames before anyone was about. Then, as no one could see the back of the house, I whitewashed the back wall. I was up the ladder doing this when I heard voices, and Jean-Pierre brought Giulia and Carlo around by the side of the house.

Hastily I climbed down, very conscious of my old clothes, well splattered with paint and whitewash.

"In the name of the Virgin, what are you doing up there, Annalisa?" Carlo demanded.

"I have to get it all clean and fresh for Giovanni to come home to next week."

"But women *never* do this sort of work," Giulia said.

"In Switzerland, women do *all* sorts of work," I replied. "I'm sorry I did not expect you, or I would have been cleaned up and ready. But come in and see what I have done."

Giulia and Carlo followed me inside, and Jean-Pierre ran in front of us crying, "Mamma painted all this."

"You mean, *you* painted the windows and walls and the furniture?" Carlo demanded.

"It was so dirty and shabby," I said apologetically. "Giulia, please do not tell your mother what I have been doing."

"She should be pleased Giovanni is getting such a hard-working wife," Carlo said sincerely, and I flushed at the words of praise. "Giulia here thinks there is no one in the world like you, and I am beginning to think she's right. I want to thank you for all you did for her and our little Romano," he said, and held out his hand. "And I want to ask you to promise to be with Giulia when the next one comes. I wish this had not happened, because I know what a bad time she has; but with you on hand, I will feel happier."

"Of course I will do all I can," I said, and my heart went out to Carlo, and I thought of him with new respect. It was good to know that he appreciated Giulia and loved her.

"We came to see if we can help you," Giulia broke in.

"Tomorrow, I'll come with old clothes and finish that whitewashing. I don't suppose I'll do it as well as you do, Annalisa, but it is not right for you to be climbing ladders," Carlo said.

I flushed and laughed. "I got up long before anyone else was awake to do the front windows," I confessed. "And no one can see me at the back."

"Well, leave the rest to me," Carlo insisted. "And tell me what I can do today. I'm quite good with a hammer and nails. Giulia said there was old furniture to be mended."

"Could you put together some window boxes to put plants in?" I asked, and Carlo stared. I explained, "In Switzerland so many houses have bright geraniums and other flowers in window boxes, that I have my heart set on having them when Giovanni comes home."

"Then show me what you want," Carlo said, and we went out to the shed, and very soon had suitable lengths of wood, a tin of old nails, and a hammer. In a short time, Carlo had the boxes nailed together, placed on the window sills, and filled with soil.

"We'll go to the flower market in Como and bring some plants with us tomorrow," Giulia said excitedly. "Carlo, when you come home will you buy me a little house like this?"

"We'll start looking even before I go back," he said, putting his arm around her. "No more living with another family for us."

"Now I'll fix something to eat," I said, going inside. "Just give me a few minutes to tidy myself."

Hastily I washed at the sink, then went upstairs, and put on a clean cotton dress.

When I came down, I proudly spread one of the freshly washed cloths on the table, with its leg propped up on a loose piece of wood, put out the collection of odd china I had brought, and gathered what food I had in my little store.

Giulia told me they had visited Giovanni, and how excited he was about coming home next week, about the surprise she had when Carlo arrived home unexpectedly, about how much she missed me, and the way the place had gone back to its normal condition since I left. And I enjoyed having someone grown-up to talk to.

I could hear Jean-Pierre chatting to Carlo in the yard, then various bangs, as if a lot of hammering was going on.

"Come and eat," I called, and together they emerged from the shed, Carlo proudly carrying a chair which he had mended, and which only needed a fresh cover on the seat; and Jean-Pierre was carrying a little stool with a new leg.

"A coat of paint and these will look like new," Carlo exclaimed. "There is enough stuff there to keep Giovanni busy for a long time, and save you buying. There is even an old bed standing up at the back behind a lot of other junk."

That was the happiest meal I had had for months, even years. Jean-Pierre insisted on sitting next to Carlo, who kept us in fits of laughter with some of his funny stories.

Giulia had grown so dear to me that I hated to see her leave. I thought she did not look well, and it was an obvious effort for her to be as gay as Carlo expected her to be. I made up my mind that I would watch Giulia as closely as I could, as the months went by.

The next morning, Giulia and Carlo brought little Eleanora and Romano with them.

"I could not leave them with Mamma and Lucia again," Giulia explained. "They think you're crazy, and said some horrible things to Carlo when he said he was coming to paint for you. Mamma said there was plenty of that to be done at home, but she has no man to help her."

"I am sorry she is so against me," I said with a sigh.

"Do not worry, Annalisa," Carlo said gaily. "Mamma Rita loves to have something to fuss about. She's never happy unless she's miserable."

His comical expression made me laugh, and I made my mind up that I would forget about Aunt Rita and her animosity. I had married Giovanni, not his family; and we need not see much of Aunt Rita, if she continued to be so hostile.

Carlo changed into his old clothes and though, as he said, he spilled almost as much whitewash as he got on the walls, the house looked wonderful when it was finished.

They had brought a basket of bright geraniums, blue lobelias, and white daisies; and Giulia and I planted them and stood back to admire the effect. I could hardly believe it was the same house as Signora Brucciani had handed over to me.

Carlo painted the gate and front door; and just as he finished, Signor Bagatti walked in, and stared in amazement.

"What a transformation," he said, wiping his forehead. "You have done all this in so short a time?"

"Signora Müller has done it all herself, except the little I have done today, Signor," Carlo said proudly. "See what she has done inside also."

Signor Bagatti walked through the living room into the kitchen, then up the bare stairs to the bedrooms.

"It's incredible," he gasped. "Never would I have believed this poor little house could look like this. I will send other tenants to see what you have done, when they start grumbling at me."

"But they might ask you to pay for the paint and whitewash," Carlo put in slyly.

"That is impossible when the rents are so low," he replied testily. "When Count Burgano comes this way, I will bring him to see the showplace on his property, Signora."

"I have no wine, Signor Bagatti," I said, "but you are welcome to coffee."

I had no intention of spending our precious money on wine for a man like him. The coffee pot stood on the stove, so that would cost me very little.

"Thank you, no, Signora," he said, bowing politely. "Coffee does not agree with me."

He accepted the money I had put aside for him, and went off with a flourish, obviously delighted at the improvements made at no cost to himself or the estate.

"I guess he has visions of the rent he will be able to charge if you ever move away. Tomorrow, I'll mend the shed roof. We'd better get it done while we have the ladder."

"But you can't spend all your leave working here. It isn't fair," I expostulated.

"He is having a marvelous time," Giulia said. "This is far better than hanging around at home, or wasting money in the wineshop."

Carlo laughed. "See what a managing wife I am going to have, now that you have set Giulia such a good example, Annalisa?"

Jean-Pierre was delighted to have someone to play with all day, so I said, "Leave Eleanor here for the night. She can sleep in the cot, and Jean-Pierre in my bed."

"We ought to get the yard fixed up a little," Carlo said, as they walked down the path, Carlo carrying Romano and Giulia walking slowly behind.

"You're sure all this is not too much for you, Giulia?" I asked, pulling her back.

"You know I love being with you, Anna," she said, and threw her arm around my shoulders. "I love you better than anyone, next to Carlo."

As I walked back into my lovely little house, my heart sang with happiness such as I had thought I could never feel again. I was not alone anymore. Giovanni and

Giulia loved me. I had Jean-Pierre, and now I had a home which I could be proud of.

I looked at the brave little flowers in the window boxes, and brought water to refresh them after the heat of the day.

The windows were shining, the whitewashed walls were gleaming in the evening sun, and the curtains were neat and fresh at the windows. Inside I looked around with satisfaction. It was still only a poor cottage; but what a change with the clean bright paint, the spotless floors, and the table covered with a cloth.

I had bought a small, tin bathtub at the secondhand shop, and pushed it into an alcove in the kitchen. I would hang a curtain up in front of it, so when buckets of water were heated on the stove, we could have a bath and keep ourselves clean.

One of the things I had found so hard to bear were the body odors of the Italians, mixed with their eternal garlic. I was determined that Giovanni and Jean-Pierre would never smell like that.

I had sanded the old sink, and it looked more presentable; but I longed for a white porcelain one, with taps which I could turn on.

Eleanor and Jean-Pierre were a grubby little pair when I called them in. I put them in the sink and they splashed happily; then after a supper of bread and milk, they fell asleep almost before they had laid down; and I went downstairs determined that before I did anything else, I would write to Dr. Margaret Roos. She had been so good to me through all the months of misery. I wanted her to share my good fortune too. I felt I could tell her that I was thanking God for this little house, and tell her how sweet and kind Giovanni, Giulia, and Carlo were to me.

When the letter was finished, I made some bright cushions out of some of the scraps I had found, and put them on the old wooden settle and the chair Carlo had mended. How gay the room was beginning to look. I would obtain some bright posters or calendar pictures, ask Carlo to put a frame around them, and hang them on the walls; then with some flowers on the table, no one could wish for a more cheerful home.

When I had time, I would weave mats for the floor, as we used to do in Switzerland, from brightly colored rags. They cost nothing but were warm and hard wearing.

Now I sat in the lamplight, mending the old sheets I had washed, and dreamed of the future. Surely Giovanni and I could be happy here. Jean-Pierre would have a good home, even if it was only a little one, and someday there would be other little brothers and sisters to play with. I loved children; and being Roman Catholics, we believed it our duty to have large families, and so bring up sons and daughters for the church.

The next day, Carlo mended the shed roof as best he could; then we tried to straighten up the yard. I insisted that Giulia sit down and watch us, and we were very merry as we puttered about.

I had decided we would have flowers in the front, so Carlo dug it over so that I could plant some seeds. In the back, I left a rough patch for Jean-Pierre to play in; then on the rest, I would grow vegetables, and thus save money. Few of my Italian neighbors bothered to grow anything, but in Switzerland every scrap of land had been precious, and vegetables were grown in summer to be canned and stored for winter. I would grow beans, cabbages, turnips, lettuce, peas, and potatoes. I hated the continual spaghetti or macaroni. Fresh vegetables would be so much better for Jean-Pierre and Giovanni.

By the time Carlo said good-bye, the yard was at least neat and tidy, even though there was no sign of the flowers and vegetables I dreamed of. I would need patience, but the hot sun would make them grow quickly if I watered them regularly.

# 9

---

AT LAST THE DAY CAME for Giovanni's homecoming, and how excited I was that morning, as I prepared to meet him. I wondered if I should order a taxi, but decided it would be too expensive. He was strong enough now to travel by bus.

When we neared our new home, I was glad of Jean-Pierre's chatter, for I was suddenly assailed with nervousness. Would Giovanni approve of what I had done? What sort of a life were we going to have? Would he ever be able to work again, or would he be at home all day?

These last weeks I had been so happy planning and working without anyone to criticize or find fault, that now I felt almost resentful that someone else was coming to share my little paradise and have the right to share in the decisions.

But no one could have been more charming than Giovanni in those first months of our marriage. He praised and admired the house and all I had done, and could hardly wait to invite his friends to show it off.

"No one else in our position has a house like this," he gloated. "Everyone who walks down the street stops to look at it. We'll always keep it like this, my darling; that is, until we can move to a much bigger home in Switzerland."

How happy those first months were, with a quiet happiness I appreciated all the more because of what I had suffered. I did not take it for granted, and I was truly grateful to Giovanni for marrying me and taking me out of the miserable conditions in his mother's house.

He was easily tired those days; and I was glad to care for him, and do all I could for his comfort His mother and sisters often visited him, but I know Aunt Rita resented the contrast in our little home and her own, and hinted that when I had a family such as she had, I would cease to be so fussy. Obviously they watched me with experienced eyes for the first sign that I was going to give Giovanni a child of his own, and before long I knew that their hopes were a reality, and I was delighted that Jean-Pierre would have a little brother or sister.

We went to church regularly and had masses said for the souls of Uncle Ernst and my parents, and secretly I prayed for Pierre. We paid what we could to the priest. I felt thankful to the blessed virgin for my home and my present happiness, and tried to obey what the priests told us.

Giovanni kept his promise, and I never saw him drunk those first months. He often had a bottle of wine with his family or friends when they visited us, and occasionally he went to the wineshop for a few hours, and I did not begrudge him this. Wine-drinking was the custom, and it was a quite life for a man to be tied at home with a woman and child all day.

Gradually as he grew stronger, he became restless. I asked him to repair some of the stuff still lying in the shed, and he enjoyed puttering about. I was amazed at how clever he was with his hands. So far we had been drawing his disability pension; it was not large, but I was economical, and I managed to make it eke out. But I knew that as the needs of our growing family increased, we would need more than this.

Giovanni had to have regular medical examinations, and he knew that before long he would be pronounced fit for at least a light job, then his pension would be reduced accordingly. He began to make plans to use the shed; and together we cleared it out, and put up racks for his tools, threw away the useless odds and ends, and either stacked or repaired the other things. It was quite a big place when it was cleared, and he agreed that it would make a good workshop.

Gradually first one and then another asked him to do some carpentry for them, sometimes in their houses, sometimes in his shed. It seemed to me that he was happy and satisfied at this time, and I felt proud and content.

All these months, Giulia had continued to visit us; but as the time came near for her confinement, I grew more and more worried. She was so pale and thin and drained of energy. I was also pregnant, but not as far along the way, and I felt strong and unhampered.

One day I told Giovanni that I was afraid for Giulia, and I wished she could come to us until the baby was born.

"But what about her other children? Will she leave them behind with Mamma? And where will she sleep?"

"Jean-Pierre can come in our room; Giulia can have her two little ones with her. She needs complete rest, and I promised Carlo I would be with her when her time comes."

"If it is what you wish, I won't object. Giulia was always my favorite sister. Lucia used to boss us around all the time; and when we were kids, Giulia and I always stuck together. She's the best of the bunch, as far as I'm concerned. Mamma won't like it, but we can't help that. I'll go myself and tell Giulia I want her to come here."

"Thank you, Giovanni," I said, kissing him. "You are so kind and good. You grow nicer every day."

He grinned sheepishly. "I can't help it when I live with you."

Two days later, he brought Giulia and her two little ones to join our household, and I insisted on Giulia's staying in bed for several days. I was so worried about her, that eventually I asked Dr. Birdella to call. I wished I could have consulted Dr. Perrini, but he was now serving in the army.

I did not like Dr. Birdella. He was a short-tempered, brusque little man, who evidently thought I was only making a fuss.

"Childbirth is natural," he snapped, when I explained how difficult a time Giulia had had when Romano was born. "Of course there is pain, but that is only for a short time. Yes, she is small, so that makes it more difficult; but you have no need to be perturbed. I will call again; but I am a very busy man, you understand."

"And a very poor doctor," I muttered under my breath as I closed the door.

Three weeks before Giulia's baby was due, she went into labor, and even Giovanni realized that what she was suffering was not normal.

For several hours I watched her, then sent him to bring Dr. Birdella immediately. I knew something was sadly wrong.

When Dr. Birdella arrived after an hour, he fumed and raged because he had not been called in sooner. He had forgotten that he had told me not to fuss, that childbirth is natural; now he knew that my fears had been realized.

For hours we battled for Giulia's life; then at last the baby was born, but it was a poor crippled, lifeless scrap, and I had no thought of trying to bring breath into its lungs. Aunt Rita and Lucia were shocked when they looked at it, and for once Aunt Rita was subdued. Even her tears were quiet, as she sat beside Giulia's bed.

Two nights later, as I sat up with Giulia, knowing in my heart that she was slipping from us, she said softly, "Annalisa, I know I am dying. Please call the priest tomorrow, so that I can go in peace, and pray for my soul when you go to church."

"Please rest," I said gently, my fingers on her pulse. "Only rest can make you stronger."

She smiled weakly. "I'll never be stronger. Poor Carlo, tell him I love him. But what about Eleanora and Romano? Annalisa, promise that when I have gone, you will keep them and bring them up like your own. Don't let them go to Mamma's house, where they will get no love or proper training. Please promise me, so that I can die happily."

"I promise," I said solemnly "For your sake, Giulia,

I will always care for them, if Carlo will let me have them."

"Now I can sleep," she said quietly, and gave a gentle sigh.

I sat on, wondering what Giovanni would say about this promise. With our own little one on the way, our family would suddenly increase to four. How were we going to provide for them all?

After about an hour, I realized that Giulia was sinking fast, and I hurried to the next room, where Aunt Rita was sleeping. I left her with Giulia, while I went downstairs and wakened Giovanni, who was stretched out on the floor.

"You must fetch the priest at once," I ordered. "Giulia is dying; we can do nothing more."

In less than an hour, Giulia had left us, and Aunt Rita collapsed with shock; so again I sent Giovanni for Dr. Birdella; then sent a message to Lucia, and the rest of the family.

Word had already gone to bring Carlo home, and how I dreaded having to tell him this awful news. We had no clear idea where he was, because when he had returned unexpectedly, and had helped me with the house, he had been on embarkation leave, and knew he was being sent to the front somewhere.

The day after Giulia died, word came that Carlo had been killed in battle. Giovanni and his family were stunned. They had little to say; and I had to take over the arrangements for Giulia's funeral, and caring for the children.

Aunt Rita insisted that Giulia's body should be taken back to her house, and buried by their own parish priest; and I willingly agreed. I was glad that the children would be away from such an ordeal. Aunt Rita said that at least Eleanora should attend her mother's funeral, but on this I was adamant. I would stay at home and look after the three children; they were too young to take part in such sorrow.

And in this Giovanni upheld me. He had accepted my resolve to keep the children until Carlo came home; but what he felt now that their father was dead, I had not dared to ask. There would be an army pension for each of them, but it was very small and would not cover all the expenses of good food and proper clothes.

Our house was small too, and with four growing children, we would be tightly packed.

When Giovanni returned from the funeral, he brought a visitor with him, who introduced herself as a relative of my mother. I remembered my mother talking about a distant cousin called Annalisa, who had become a nun, and many years ago had been sent to Italy to help found schools and hospitals. Now she was in her late sixties, a tall, softspoken, pale-faced woman.

As she greeted me, she took both my hands and held them while she looked in my face. "At long last I have met my namesake," she said. "Do you know that your parents named you after me? That was the name by which I was baptised, but now in the church I am called 'Madre Ignatia.' It is a long time since anyone called me Annalisa."

"But how did you find me?" I asked in bewilderment.

"I have just moved to this district. Father Pietro mentioned the sad tragedies which had happened to the Müller family, and I remembered Ernst had come to live somewhere near Como. I made inquiries and met Giovanni at the funeral of his poor sister. I asked if anyone knew anything about you, and was amazed to learn that you are here in Italy, married to Giovanni."

"How pleased I am that he brought you home. It will be so good to hear what you can tell me about my mother. So often I have wished I could remember her better."

"And these are the children, yours and Giulia's?"

"Yes, this is Jean-Pierre, and these are Eleanora and Romano. Now they are all *our* children. Please, let me make you a meal."

"Nothing to eat, only coffee, please," she replied. "Giovanni is very upset, perhaps you should go to him first."

I went out to the shed and found him sitting on the

bench, his face deathly white, staring blankly before him.

I put my arms around his shoulders, and put my face against his. "Dearest, come in and rest," I said gently. "You have had a great strain today. Please go to bed, and let me bring you a little supper."

"But I cannot do that while Madre Ignatia is here."

"She understands, Giovanni. She would not have you inconvenienced because of her. In a strange way, I have the feeling that God sent her today to help us just now. She is so kind, and she is our own flesh and blood."

Like a child, he allowed me to lead him inside, and I explained to Madre Ignatia that I felt he ought to rest.

"May God comfort you, Giovanni," she said, putting her hand on his arm. "We cannot understand His ways; there is so much suffering in the world, but we must have faith to trust Him."

I saw Giovanni lie down; then I gave the children some supper, washed them, and put them to bed. They were very quiet and subdued. Even their little minds sensed some tragedy hanging over them, and the appearance of Madre Ignatia overawed them.

I took some wine and rolls up to Giovanni; then Madre Ignatia and I sat down to our coffee, and to a quiet talk together.

"Your mother wrote to me for many years," she began. "I still have a prayer book printed in German and Italian, which she sent me almost twenty years ago, God rest her soul. Often she asked me to pray that you might be guided into the path I had chosen, but the ways of the Lord are many. The convent is only an easy way for some to know God, but the way through tribulations is surely the most rewarding. By carrying our cross as Jesus did, we will be nearer to Him and He to us. Tell me when and how you came here, Annalisa. Giovanni told me only a very little."

So, very shyly and haltingly I told her my sad little story, afraid of what this woman, who had lived so long away from the sins and temptations of the world, would say to me.

When I had finished, her fine gray eyes were wet with tears. "How you have suffered, child," she said softly. Now God has given you another husband and a home; and from what I have already heard, I am proud of what you are doing. May I come to see you again? I feel I have not much time left to me, and it is good to find once again someone belonging to my own family."

"It will make me *very* proud," I replied. "I have few friends, and do not fit into the Italian way of life."

She nodded. "Yes, Italians are very different from the Swiss; but they have many good points, nevertheless. Now I must go. God bless you and this house, Annalisa. I will pray for you in the hard task you have ahead. You will need great patience, but the Lord will help you."

After I had tidied the room, I went up to Giovanni, my heart comforted. He lay awake, and I held him close to me; then as he burst into sobs, I tried to soothe him.

"Giulia and Carlo were the best of the lot," he said brokenly. "Why did God allow this to happen? What had they done wrong?"

"Nothing. They're victims of this wicked war," I said bitterly. "If they had been able to live in their own home in a normal way, probably Giulia would not have died. Certainly Carlo wouldn't have been killed."

"Then why doesn't God—if there is a God—not stop all war?" he burst out.

Gropingly I tried to tell him what Dr. Margaret had told me, explaining that if God stopped war, He would have to stop man's free will to choose good and evil; war was caused by man's sin and greed, and the innocent must suffer with the guilty, but that did not mean that we personally should be wicked. We would be judged by what each of us had done, not on what others had brought into the world. We could not stop the war, nor prevent Carlo being killed, nor Giulia's dying; but we could do our part to put some of the wrong right by caring for their children and seeing that they had a chance to grow up decently. Had I been a Christian then, I could have pointed out that God had a good purpose for everything He let happen.

"It sounds good, Annalisa, but then you are far more clever than I am. I can't see the point of trying to live decently, and why bring kids into a world like this?"

"We cannot alter the world, but we can make one little bit of it as decent as we can," I said.

"My darling, how sweet you are. I'm not good enough for you," he said, as he stroked my hair. "What would I do without you? Suppose you die like Giulia, when our baby is born? Who will care for all of us?"

"Hush, don't talk like that," I said. "I am well and strong; nothing will go wrong. Millions of babies are born every year, and very few mothers die. Giulia ought to have had greater care and a much longer period of rest, before she had the strain of another baby."

"But our priests won't allow that."

"I know that the church says one must not try to regulate one's family, but it's hard to know what's right in this matter. But you have talked enough. You must sleep now. I will get you one of the pills I have hidden for such an emergency."

I brought him the tablet and some water, and he pulled me down to him.

"My darling, you are so wonderful," he said brokenly. "I could not live without you."

I crept downstairs, and for a few minutes, sat by the dying embers in the stove. There was so much to think about, and I had been so busy all day.

I wept for Giulia and Carlo, and for Aunt Rita who had had so many shocks recently. I thanked God for sending Madre Ignatia into my life again to comfort me. I felt that here was someone so much older and wiser who would help and advise me, and at present I needed someone to turn to. Giovanni was still a sick man in many ways and utterly dependent on me for encouragement, so that I felt I had four children instead of three; and sometimes the load was heavy. If only I had known God in a personal relationship, I could have tapped His resources for the strength I needed. Instead, I was on my own.

When I crept upstairs, I peeped into the children's

room. Eleanora lay in a small bed, the covers kicked off and her dark curly hair spread out over the pillow; Jean-Pierre and Romano were in their cribs, and I thought, *Already Jean-Pierre is growing too tall for his crib, we will have to get another bed somehow, and anyway, soon I will need his crib for the new baby.*

How sweet and innocent they all looked in sleep. What a responsibility lay before me. Without putting it into actual thoughts, I knew in my mind that I would always have to share the heavier end of the load. Giovanni was a good husband, but not a strong one. He would need constantly propping up and reassuring.

He was fast asleep when I crept into bed, and my thoughts were very tender as I listened to his heavy breathing. He and I had gone through deep waters these last months. Life had not been easy, but being needed made up to me for many things. I thought of Giovanni as I had first known him—carefree, lighthearted, easily amused; now all the joy of life seemed to have left him. He was docile and apparently content, but far too subdued for his years. *Something more the war has to account for*, I thought bitterly. *How much longer is it going on, and how much more can we stand?*

# 10

NEXT MORNING, Giovanni was listless and unhappy. I suggested that he rest and not try to work, but he decided he must go to see his mother and the rest of the family. I did not try to dissuade him, but I hated to see him go. I knew that again the neighbors would congregate, there would be much wine flowing, and Aunt Rita would try to work on his sympathies.

He did not come back that night, and I waited up for him long after our usual bedtime. When he returned the next day, he was taciturn and morose. He made no apology for leaving me alone, but I knew that he must have been drunk the night before and unfit to come home.

From that day there was a marked change in his attitude toward me. Sometimes he was passionate and affectionate, but often he was irritable, and I needed all the patience I could muster to live at peace with him.

He went frequently to Aunt Rita's; and whenever he came back, I knew that his mother had been working on him to come home; but I was determined that come what may, I would never go back to live in such a household.

Then one day he came home in a furious temper. I had never seen him in such a rage, and I was afraid he would do the children some harm, so I hurried them up to their room.

"Now tell me what is the matter?" I asked calmly.

"You ask what is the matter? *Everything* is the matter. Today Lucia has been told that her miserable skunk of a husband, Giorgio, has deserted from the army. He has disappeared, and now she will get no money for herself or the children. If I could get my hands on his fat neck, I'd break it for him as fast as I would break a twig. Papa never wanted Lucia to marry him, the ugly, fat gigolo, but Lucia would not listen; now he has gone. If he is found he will be courtmartialed, and all the time Lucia and Mamma have to suffer."

"But where has he gone?"

"With another woman, you may be sure," he replied scathingly. "He never could let women alone, and Lucia knew it, but she shut her eyes to his dirty little affairs."

"Poor Lucia," I said sadly. "It would have been better to hear he had been killed like Carlo."

"Quick killing is too good for scum like Giorgio. Slow torture is what he deserves."

All day he brooded; then he burst out, "We will have

to go back to live with Mamma. She says she cannot live without a man in the house."

"No, Giovanni, this house is ours; we are staying here," I said firmly but quietly.

His face grew crimson. "I am the husband; if I say we move, then we move."

"Then I will not go with you," I said, though my limbs were shaking.

He stared at me, then dropping some of his bluster said, "How would you live here if I did not give you money?"

"I don't know, but somehow I'll find work to support the children and myself. I will never take them back to that sort of life."

"You think you're too good for my family, don't you?" he shouted angrily.

"Your mother hates me," I replied. "And how much peace and rest would you get in that crowded house?"

"We managed before you came," he snapped.

"You have listened to your mother until she has turned you against me; but believe me, Giovanni, I mean what I say. I will borrow money and go back to Switzerland, if that is the only alternative."

"So that is all you care about me," he shouted.

"I care so much about you and our baby, who will soon be here, that I will never return to what I suffered all those months before we were married."

Suddenly, as so often happened, his mood changed, and he held out his arms. "Anna, my beloved, what have I done? How could I talk to you like that? I love you; you must never leave me. How could you think of going to Switzerland?"

"I only told you to show how determined I am to keep our own home. We were so happy, Giovanni, before Giulia died. What has happened to us?"

"It's all my fault," he muttered. "Forgive me, *cara mia*."

"It's because you have gone home too much, and there has been too much wine." I said bravely, for I was

determined not to be browbeaten. "You've done so little
work lately, and we need money for so many things."

"I'll start all over again tomorrow, Anna. We'll be
happy once more."

And on the surface, things went on much as before;
but I knew that the quiet, inner content of those first
months was shattered. I did not love Giovanni as a wife
ought to love, and now I knew there was an instability
in him which could wreck our happiness.

For the next few days he worked hard, and more orders than he could cope with were pouring in. At his last
medical examination he had been told that he had been
upgraded, and his pension would be cut accordingly; so
it was necessary that he should make a sufficient living
to keep the family in food and other essentials.

He had started going to the wineshop for an hour
each evening, and I dared not remonstrate, but I hated
the thought of our precious money being wasted.

When our baby boy was born, Giovanni was once
more an attentive, devoted husband for a few weeks. I
called our son Ernst after his grandfather, and Giovanni
was proud of him. He was a beautiful baby, very fair
and long limbed.

"Not much Italian about him," Giovanni said one day
as he looked at him. "I guess he's just about all Müller."

Then he amazed me by saying, "I've been thinking
that we ought to call Jean-Pierre 'Giovanni.' It will be
easier when he goes to school, and what is more natural
than that our eldest son should be called after me?"

For a few seconds, I dropped my eyes. I did not want
Giovanni to see the hurt in them at the thought of dropping the name Pierre had chosen for his son; but I knew
that what he said made good sense, and I was grateful.

"That is a kind thought," I said, smiling at him. "Although sometimes we will get mixed up between Papa
Giovanni and little Giovanni."

So from that time, Pierre's son became "Giovanni" to
other people, but to me he was always Jean-Pierre in my
secret thoughts. Someday I would tell him about his own

father, and maybe he would want to take back his real name.

During that first year of baby Ernst's life, the war ended; and a weary, tired remnant of men returned home to find conditions were even worse than when they went away. Most of their jobs had been taken by other people, money was scarce, food expensive; and there was a lot of talk about emigrating to other countries, where people could have a better chance of earning a living.

Giovanni was fortunate. He was an excellent craftsman, and his business boomed. People needed a lot of repairs and rebuilding done, and soon he was able to employ first one man, then two.

But he became increasingly difficult to live with. Almost every year I had another child, or sometimes it was a miscarriage, for which I was grateful, as it meant one less mouth to feed. Our little house was bursting at the seams, but Giovanni refused to move; so after a great deal of persuasion, he put up another hut in the garden, and the older children slept there.

Gradually I came to realize that the man I was living with bore no resemblance to the one I thought I had married, and only my children kept me tied to him.

Of course it was impossible to hide my feelings altogether. Night after night, he came home either in a violent temper, or in a drunken stupor. I did not know which was the worst. He became violently jealous and used to accuse me of having affairs with men to whom I had never even spoken. He said I was cold and unresponsive, and what man wanted such a wife?

With such a quickly growing family, we were constantly in need of money. Giovanni could have built up a good business; but as the years went on, he spent more and more time in the tavern. At first I tried working with him, in the hope that this would help him settle down. I learned carpentry; but as soon as he realized I could use his tools, he would leave me to finish the jobs, while he boasted to his cronies about what a clever wife he had. When our family became so large that I could not spend time in the workshop, he employed other workmen; but often they did not know what to do, and they did not dare go to the tavern to ask Giovanni, because of his furious temper.

I tried to earn a little money by working for the neighbors, knitting, nursing those who were ill, or writing letters for them, as so many were unable to read and write; but Giovanni was furious every time he knew I had been away from the house, and these people were so poor that I hated to take even a few lire from them.

It was an impossible life. I had been used to something so different, that I felt degraded morally and materially. I knew that many other women were treated in the same way, that they received beatings when their husbands came home drunk; but I was unable to accept such conditions as normal. I had nobody except Madre Ignatia to talk to; no one else would understand how I felt. Often we were short of food, and I went to bed hungry, because I gave my share to the growing children. I kept them clean, but how often I wept as I had to send them to school in wornout clothes, and barefooted, because I could not afford to buy them shoes. Giovanni kept all the money he earned, and doled out the smallest amounts for necessities. He so often accused me of wanting to leave him and go back to Switzerland, that I believe he intentionally kept money from me.

And of course, he often upbraided me with the fact that he was bringing up another man's child. How hard it was to keep quiet during these tirades; yet if I answered back, he became so infuriated that he often struck me, and I would be unable to go out because of the bruises on my face.

I was a stranger and a foreigner to these people among whom we lived. I believe they resented me, because in spite of everything, I still tried to preserve a semblance of decency. For years I struggled on; my only hope was in the children. I had no other reason to live. For them I wanted a better life. I was strict with them, and taught them to be honest and reliable, and encouraged them to study as much as possible. They were afraid of their father; and when they grew older, they secretly despised him.

I tried to find comfort in the church, but so much of it did not make sense. The priests continually demanded money from the people, although many of them were living in absolute poverty. I could not reconcile the fact that the churches were filled with statues adorned with gold and priceless jewels, while the people did not have enough to eat.

Madre Ignatia was my only real friend and solace. The nuns made dresses for my children; and often she sent for me, knowing by now that I needed to get away from my miserable home for a few hours.

But this made Giovanni furious. He said I talked about him to her, telling her what a bad husband he was, instead of letting her know that I was only a "pretend" wife, who did not love or obey her husband, and that I had only married him to make a home for my child.

So to prevent such scenes, I pretended I did not want to visit her when she invited me to go to the convent, but asked him to go in my place. She was an old woman, and he too was her relative. And my plan worked. He thought I did not wish to go, so he sent me. Gradually the children and I learned that the only way we could get what we wanted was to pretend to want the opposite; then out of sheer contradiction, Giovanni would command us to do that very thing.

During the years that followed, Aunt Rita died; the rest of the girls married; and Lucia disappeared with her children. Somehow Giorgio had contacted her, and she had gone back to him, but we had no trace of them.

Eventually we moved to a bigger house in Verona. By this time, I had five children of my own and Lucia's two; so I was glad for a bigger house, though it needed so much cleaning, that I was almost in despair. But the children were big enough to help me; I had trained the girls to work properly, and together we made the dilapidated old house a decent place.

I was determined that my children would receive all

the education they could, and one of the good things which Benito Mussolini ordered was the building of schools. When children reached the age of eleven, they could choose between an industrial school, where they learned carpentry, engineering, printing, etc.; a commercial school, where they learned typewriting and accountancy; or a scientific school, where they trained as teachers and scientists.

Automatically the boys became members of the Balillas, the youth guard of fascism. How important the little boys felt in their uniforms, which consisted of a pair of fieldgreen trousers, a black shirt, and a black fez with a long tassel which swayed to the rhythm of the march.

All the children were now compelled to go to school; there was no dropping out, as there had been in their parents' time.

My children loved school, and I helped them with their homework, or sometimes I learned with them.

When Jean-Pierre now known as little Giovanni and Ernst, my two boys, and Romano, grew old enough, Giovanni insisted that they should learn carpentry, so that they could join him in the business when they finished school; but they hated the idea of working for him, and waited for the time when they could join the army.

I longed to find some way of earning money myself, but he would not hear of my doing anything. He expected complete submission from a wife. She was to be his slave, to bear his children, to cook his food, and to obey his every command.

Even now I can scarcely bear to recall those years of utter misery and degradation. I dreaded the time when the boys would leave home; because then the girls and I would have no one to protect us from their father's violent rages, when he seemed to lose all control of himself.

I thought at last I had finished childbearing, and my family was complete; then four years after René was born, to my dismay, I found I was pregnant once more. I was so exhausted and tired of the life I had to live, that I longed to die and be at rest.

When my little Yvonne was born, I was so desperately ill that I was rushed to the maternity hospital; and the baby had to be taken by a caesarean section. I had a long rest in the hospital before I was considered fit to go back to the constant struggle of bringing up such a big family, plus a rather delicate baby girl.

Maybe Giovanni had received a shock and realized how much he depended on me, for he was more considerate for a few months.

However, as Yvonne grew stronger and I was able to cope, he soon forgot, and life went on as before.

Little Giovanni and Romano were working in the shop with him, but Ernst, Giovanni's own son, refused to join them when he left school. The other two were more submissive, but Ernst had too much of his father's stubbornness in his makeup, and he and Giovanni were continually at loggerheads. He was determined that as soon as he could, he would join the army and get away from home.

Giovanni hated to see me reading; he could not bear to see me even glancing at a magazine. We had no books, except those that the children brought home from school; but sometimes, Ernst, who had a paper route after school and on weekends, brought home old newspapers for me, and I eagerly read them in secret. My mind was starved for contact with anyone who thought of anything beyond wine and polenta, or the shallow little happenings of the neighbors.

After Madre Ignatia died, there was no one I could talk to. Even our parish priest had no time for us; we were too poor.

I had long felt the inconsistencies of the church. The poor people tried to obey what they were taught; but too often the priests themselves were selfish, failing creatures, and poor representatives of God on earth.

There were some who, I feel, genuinely knew the Lord and were true ministers, and tried to alleviate suffering; but many made an obvious distinction between the rich and the poor.

A widow who lived near me had tuberculosis, and had to have frequent spells in a sanatorium. She needed help very badly, especially to get a job for her fifteen-year-old boy. Next to her house lived a rich, elderly bachelor, who also had TB. Almost every day the priest went to see the old man; but he never once visited the poor widow or did anything to help her son to obtain work, although the mother begged for his assistance many times.

At that time, Roman Catholics in Italy regarded a priest as the representative of the Almighty, our Father in heaven, and we hated to be faced with the human side of them. They were placed on a pedestal and expected to do no wrong. They interfered in what most Protestants would regard as private problems, condemning those who did not have children frequently or did not give continually to the church; people were afraid to disobey, lest they call down the curse of the church upon themselves.

In every church there were thousands of dollars worth of gold and silver rings, necklaces, bracelets, and jewels of all description, adorning cases, shrines, and statues. As I looked at them, I often thought, *Surely God would be better pleased if this useless wealth were used to alleviate the poverty and sufferings of many of His people.* But of course, I never dared express such feelings aloud.

Tension was again in the air. Mussolini was rousing the country, rallying the people behind him, training his army and air force. He introduced many things which helped the ordinary people; and naturally, they hailed him as their great leader. The priests preached continually against communism, but listening to them, I felt that often they used this as a threat to demand greater faithfulness to the church, and of course, more money.

I often thought of what I had learned from Dr. Margaret's New Testament. The teachings of our Lord Jesus were to glorify God, to love one's neighbors, and do all the good you could to others, and live at peace.

These were not the teachings I heard when I went to church. "Bring your alms to the church, for we need to rebuild," was always the most important part of the service. Then looking over the "flock" before him with his piercing eyes, our priest would name certain people who were not in church, and had not been there for several weeks. Therefore they were "communists," that is, enemies of the church and enemies of society; and it would be better for them if they had never been born. Often those same people were ashamed to come to church, because they had no decent clothes or shoes to wear. Did the priest care?

His wrath and condemnation never included the rich. The poor who failed to pay their dues and appear at church regularly were "communists"; and during his yearly tour of houseblessing after Easter, the priest would carefully avoid those particular dwellings. The members of the family waiting for the Lord's blessing would see him pass without deigning to enter or look their way. No wonder bitterness and rebellion against such treatment filled their hearts.

Often the same thing happened during processions. When a so-called "communist" family lived along the road where the processions had passed for as long as people could remember, the priest ordered a change of route. "God, in the holy Eucharist, must not be profaned by the sight of communists."

For myself, I could find no comfort in the empty rituals; they were so full of blatant contradictions. I could not accept the dogmas as blindly as so many others appeared to do. The priests' words never had the ring of truth that Dr. Roos' words had, about God's love.

One day Mussolini came to our town, and we welcomed him with much cheering and flag-waving. All the school children marched to their allotted places; and we adults crowded wherever we could, to see our hero.

He cut a fine figure in his uniform with many decorations on his chest; and as his voice carried over the crowds, we were beside ourselves with excitement. Here at last, we felt, was someone who cared about his country and the ordinary people in it.

He was a great orator, and as he spoke of the right of the Italian people to have a place in the sun, of the need to stop the emigration of our sons to other countries because there was not space enough or work enough in the beloved motherland, we were carried away with his rhetoric.

"Ethiopia is the place we will go to conquer and civilize," he thundered. "Our soldiers will be true sons of those Roman soldiers who glorified the name of Rome, and brought the blessings of culture and civilization to countries all over the world."

The huge crowd cheered wildly. "Viva il Duce!" "Down with Haile Selassie!" they roared, but some of the older people were less enthusiastic; many of them had been in Ethiopia as soldiers when they were young, and they remembered how many had been buried around Makale and other places, and they feared for their sons.

It was only two weeks later that Mussolini declared war on Ethiopia, with the result that many countries imposed sanctions against Italy, and refused to send her necessary imports. Only Germany with Hitler at its head, supported Mussolini. This was the beginning of the Rome-Berlin Axis.

Mussolini had built up fascism in Italy; but for many years there had been constant friction between the regular army, headed by the king, and the fascist army led by Mussolini, especially as the members of the latter were paid much more than the regulars.

Once, an officer of the regular army told me that "Any loud-mouthed fascist, without any academic training, can become an officer in Mussolini's army; while officers of the regular army have to have years of training, and be college graduates."

The regular army had never interfered in domestic details, but as the fascists grew in power, no one was safe. If anyone dared to disagree with their doctrines, he was arrested or refused a job or his family made to suffer. Gradually fear crept in, and no one trusted anyone anymore. There were spies and informants everywhere.

I was sure at the time that Mussolini for the most part had no idea of what was actually taking place. When anyone wrote to him about the wrongs which were being perpetrated, he ordered the local authorities to straighten out such irregularities immediately. But then the complainant would be called before them and threatened with what would happen if he ever dared to write and complain to the "Duce" again.

I was certain Mussolini would not have allowed so much pressure and abuse to go on, but the wrong men were seizing power which fascism gave them, and using it for their own ends, I thought.

When all the wives of Italy gave their wedding rings to be sold to support the war in Ethiopia, most of those gold rings disappeared into the pockets of the local fascists. Much was whispered about the scandal, but it was quickly hushed up by the restrictions on the press. When at long last the war in Ethiopia ended, and the king of Italy was once more crowned, people realized with sorrow what a tragedy this Ethiopian campaign had been. Italy had lost her empire, and conditions were no better; but at the time, the majority of the people worshipped Mussolini, as the Germans worshipped Hitler.

# *11*

◆

AFTER MY LITTLE YVONNE was born, before I left the hospital, I overheard a doctor saying that someone was needed to translate a special medical report by a German doctor. I asked if they would allow me to translate it, if there was no one else to do it. Professor Angelino looked at me in surprise, then said, "You can help Doctor Bianco, who is supposed to know a little German."

That afternoon he came armed with the medical report, a small medical dictionary, a pen, and paper; but as soon as he had all these spread out on the table, he was called away by a nurse and was absent almost two hours. I started reading and found it quite easy to translate. By the time Dr. Bianco returned, I had already translated part of the report.

He read over what I had written, then said, "I did not think that a lay person could understand and translate a medical report as well as this. Please continue with the remainder; but do only a little at a time, so that you do not get overtired."

It took me about three days to finish it. Evidently it met with Professor Angelino's approval, for he sent for me and said, "I have been wondering about you ever since you first came to our notice several years ago. We all know that your husband has disregarded our advice to the point where you almost lost your life. Evidently it is beyond him to regard a wife in any other light than a machine to produce children for him. I sensed that you were very different. Obviously you have a good education, and abilities which could be used to help your family. Stop being afraid of your husband and allowing him to dictate to you. You can get a well-paid job easily. Many offices would be glad to employ you. I, myself, will need you often, so may other doctors on this staff, as we work now in close conjunction with German medical men. I will speak to someone who may be able to give you permanent work. Remember, you cannot go on living as you have done all these years. A dead mother is of no use to her children, nor is a starving one, who thinks that her part of the food should go to her children."

I knew that he was right. For years, I had longed to do work which would not only benefit the family, but allow me to "think" once more. I made up my mind that as soon as I could find someone reliable to look after my children, I would look around for some suitable occupation. I knew that Giovanni would put every obstacle in my way, but my determination was growing. For twenty years I had submitted to him and put up with a life of misery, ill-treatment, and frustration, but my will was not dead. I always felt compelled to rise above the situation around me. Yet it seemed that I was unable to raise myself high enough. Later I was to realize that only God's Son could give the true freedom that always eluded my grasp.

It was some months later when I noticed an advertisement in an old newspaper Ernst had brought in for me.

"The Ministry of Transport and Communications has opened a Concourse for interpreters with the knowledge of Italian, French, and German languages. All Italian citizens under the age of forty-five may apply, sending their birth certificates, and other necessary documents of qualifications, to the above Ministry before June 30, 1938. The daily wage for those accepted would be 50 lire."

I read this advertisement again and again. The paper was already two weeks out of date; was there time for me to apply? Would Giovanni allow me to even try for such a position?

I could speak fluent German, French, and Italian, so I had the necessary qualifications. I had taught my children German and French, so I had never lost my knowledge of these languages. When Giovanni was not present, we used to enjoy talking in something other than Italian.

If I asked my husband to allow me to apply, he would refuse, because he always went against anything I wanted to do.

Finally I folded the paper very small, and put it on the table beside his plate, with the advertisement in full view.

As he glanced down at his food, he idly scanned the paper; then he said, "Did you read this ad? Why don't you try for it? We could use that money."

I could hardly believe my ears, but I pretended that I was not interested and had too much work to do at home.

"Always you grumble about your work," he replied

angrily. "The girls are old enough to help. They can look after the baby. You turn down the chance of fifty lire a day, when you are forever moaning about not having any money. Send in your application at once, do you hear me?"

"Very well," I replied meekly. "But I will need to send to Switzerland for my birth certificate and other papers."

"Then send off tonight."

I could have shouted for joy. Here at last was a glimpse through an open doorway into a new life for myself and my children. That night I wrote to Switzerland; then when I had all the documents and letters of recommendation gathered together, I sent them off to Rome with a heart full of hope. When the answer came, it was like a physical blow. My application had arrived too late, but I would be given another opportunity the following year.

In May 1939, I received an invitation from the Ministry to forward my documents and application form. This year, however, English was also required. I stared at the paper. I knew no English; what could I do? Were all my hopes to be shattered again?

There were six months before the examinations, and I made up my mind that somehow, I would learn English before the appointed date, so again I sent my application to Rome.

I had tried hard to be a good wife to Giovanni and a good mother to our children, but I could not go on in this intellectually starved situation any longer. No matter what I suffered, how hard I had to struggle, I would seize this opportunity before me. God had shown me a way. I had prayed so often to be delivered from my awful bondage; this, I felt, was His answer.

I knew that I could expect beatings and black eyes from Giovanni if he saw me studying; but I was willing to risk anything, if I could hold up my head once more, and feel that what I was doing would benefit my family.

The next day, I went to one of my children's teachers and asked for her advice. When she heard what I was trying to do, she became so excited that she hugged me, saying she knew that I would succeed. The teachers admired the way I struggled to keep my family clean, and encouraged them to study, she told me.

One of her sons was a professor, and she was sure he could find an English grammar book which he would not use until the next school year.

When she put that grammar into my hands the next day, it is almost impossible to explain how I felt. Her confidence in me was my first inspiration; and as I pressed the book to my breast, the tears poured down my cheeks. This was the key which I believed would open the doors of my prison of poverty.

I would fight, no matter how hard it was. I was forty years old, and had ten children to care for, the youngest one only a year old; but life could begin again for me.

At first Giovanni seemed glad about my studying. He understood that to obtain the money he wanted from me, I needed to learn English; so he did not interfere, and I gave every spare minute I could to studying. I could not attend a language school; but with the other three languages I already knew, and with the help of the excellent grammar, after two months of hard study, I started a diary in English.

One afternoon, Yvonne was playing on the floor, the older boys and girls were working or at school, and I was studying in the kitchen at the table, when I heard my husband stumble up the path. I knew by his footsteps that he was intoxicated. The door was open, and as he caught sight of me, he flew into a furious temper. Rushing forward, he grabbed the grammar, inkstand, and copybook, and threw them out of the door. "I will kill you if ever I see you wasting your time over that stupid junk again," he yelled. "I know why you want this job. It's so that you can get money and leave me and the children. You think I'm not good enough for you, that you are so much cleverer than I am; but I will show you who is boss in this house. Write and cancel your application, or I'll thrash you until you cannot move."

I stood there staring at his red, stupid face with its blazing eyes; and I did not care what he did to me.

Yvonne started to scream, and I bent down and grasped her in my arms.

"Kids yelling everywhere, day and night," Giovanni bawled. "There's no peace for a man anywhere. What sort of a home is this, with a woman who sits with her nose in a book all day, muttering to herself like an old witch, and kids always wanting money to spend?"

With an oath he turned and lurched outside. Obviously he was going back to the only solace he knew. As he went, he kicked disdainfully at the book and broken ink bottle.

I did not weep; my heart felt too cold and murderous, and I was almost frightened at the terrible sense of revulsion and hatred which filled me. I comforted Yvonne, then went outside and tenderly gathered together the torn pages which were splattered all over with ink.

Very carefully I used bleach to cleanse as much as possible, then tried to stick the pages together, so that I could use it once more. Nothing was going to stop me now. Beatings and black eyes did not terrify me any longer.

I did not find the English language too difficult. It was quite easy to understand the composition of a sentence; and after I had learned a few pages by heart, I started making up sentences of my own. I had a good memory; and as I went about my ordinary household tasks, my brain was going over and over the words I had learned.

After Giovanni's explosion, I devised a simple plan. I put the grammar in the open table drawer; and before me on the table, I kept some potatoes or other vegetables ready for peeling. Immediately when I heard my husband's footsteps, I simply closed the drawer and started peeling the potatoes. And at night as soon as I heard him snoring, I got up and went downstairs to the kitchen, where I studied until my eyes would not keep open any longer.

My children were marvelous during this time. They

stood guard while I studied, and as soon as they saw their father coming, helped me hide my books.

For a little while after his outburst, Giovanni did not realize that I was defying him, and in spite of his threatenings was continuing in my own way. When he did realize it, he hunted until he found the grammar, then tore it to pieces, and beat me unmercifully.

Next day my children put together the few centesimi they had saved, and bought me a new grammar. This happened four times during the five months I studied. But now I did not worry if I had to go out to the market and let the neighbors see my bruised face. Word of what I was trying to do went around the neighborhood, and first one then another let me know that they were proud of me for having the will to stand up against my husband.

At the end of November, I went to see the English teacher of the Berlitz School, because I wanted to know if my English was any good, or if I were simply deluding myself and wasting my time and energy.

I asked her to examine my English diary, and I watched her face closely as she read it. "I am utterly amazed. Are you sure that you never learned English before you came to Italy?"

"No, I knew no English before I started on this grammar," I replied.

"During my twenty years of teaching, I have never known anyone to learn so fast and so well, and you had no one to teach you. You do not need lessons. Your written work is excellent, but try to find someone with whom you can practice speaking English, to help with the pronunciation."

I was so happy and proud as I left the school, that people turned around to look at me. I felt as if I could not stop to walk sedately through the streets. I almost ran the four miles home to tell my family. Of course, this was only the first step; but it was the most important one, and it showed me that I could still have faith in myself.

The tests were due to be held in Rome in December.

How I was to get there without Giovanni's permission, I did not know; but I would manage it somehow.

When Christmas passed, and still I had heard nothing from the Ministry, I wrote asking if my application had been overlooked.

The reply came back, "Because of the present international situation, the date of the tests has had to be postponed."

Hitler had by this time invaded Poland, and the whole world was once more in the grip of international tension. No one knew what would be the outcome of this invasion.

I was bitterly disappointed, but I determined to continue studying, so that I would be all the more prepared for the tests when they did come.

A few months later, I was invited to call at the office of labor. Professor Angelino had recommended me, so he had not forgotten his promise.

As a test, several sentences were dictated to me in which foreign names of people and streets frequently occurred. Then I was given some documents concerning Italian emigrants to France and Germany, which I had to translate. As a result, I was offered a post in the office of labor as a translator and foreign relations clerk.

But first I must somehow make Giovanni allow me to accept this position which I coveted so much. To do this, I wrote out a report stating the absolute necessity for me to take this job, and took it to the chief of police, asking for his help and protection. He called the police station nearest to our home, and asked the marshal to go to my husband and tell him that he, the chief, wanted me to go to work, and that my husband must not interfere in any way. This was a national emergency, and people with my qualifications were scarce.

By the time I reached my home, my husband had been interviewed by the marshal; and he had plenty to say, but did not lay his hands on me. As I did not trouble to answer, he said, "All right, you go to work, but at the end of the month I will come to your office and get your wages."

This is just what he did, but the marshal heard about it and paid Giovanni another visit. He told him that as I had earned the money, it was mine, and that he should be ashamed to force his wife to go out to work, when he could earn enough to keep his family, if he did not spend so much money treating his friends and himself in the tavern.

Italian workers had often been employed by foreign industrialists, and in the years prior to World War II, a great many workers went to Germany on contracts of six or twelve months. The labor office of Verona was one of the most important offices in Italy for this purpose, as they dealt with so many of these returned workers when their contract was finished; and they reenlisted others for new contracts.

It was my job to ensure that any of these workers who had been forced to return because of ill health, or for family reasons, got all the money due to them from their German employers. In fact, I was there to act as advisor and helper to any who had problems over German employment.

When Hitler invaded Poland, we feared that Italy would be involved before long; and so it proved. Italy entered the war, and more and more workers were sent to Germany to work in the arms factories.

Young Giovanni and Romano received their call-up papers, and a few months later, Ernst volunteered.

I felt that I was living all over again those terrible months in Switzerland before World War I. Again we went through the tension and agony of facing a future of sorrow and danger. In those days, the memory of Pierre was seldom far from my mind. War had taken him from me; now it was taking his son.

Giovanni did not seem to care what happened to any of us. He talked loudly of the exploits he and his friends had engaged in when he was young and in the army, but no one took any notice of him.

He did not belong to any particular party, but he liked to pretend that he knew everything; and because he was always willing to stand drinks for everyone who

would applaud him, he was used to an audience who
egged him on to make a fool of himself. In the tavern he
might be regarded as a good companion, but at home he
was a bad-tempered, domineering bully. None of us ever
knew what his reactions would be. If we did a certain
thing as he demanded one day, the next day it was all
wrong and must be done in the opposite way.

Long ago I had given up trying to understand him,
but I had submitted for the sake of a little peace for the
children.

I knew how glad young Giovanni, Ernst, and Romano were to get away from his tyranny; and the girls
were longing for the day when they too could escape.

One day just before war broke out, a group of "black
shirts" (fascists) came in search of one of my husband's
friends. I had seen him in the workshop a little while before, but I knew these fascists only brought trouble; so
in the worst Italian possible, I told them I did not understand what they wanted.

However, they eventually found the man they were
looking for, and in front of a large crowd, forced him to
swallow a half-pint of castor oil, telling him that next
time it would be deportation to a labor camp if he continued to preach socialism, which was really communism. Even this did not make him keep quiet, and later
he was arrested, and for two years he was in a labor
camp somewhere in Italy. When he came home, he had
very little to say until the war was over.

This had some effect on my husband and his cronies,
who had talked so much when they had a few drinks;
but nothing made Giovanni change toward his own family.

How I hated to let my boys go; yet how proud I felt
as I looked at them in their uniforms. It had been such a
struggle to bring them up, but no one, I felt, had a bet-
ter-looking family than mine. They would have gone a
long way if only they had had a better education and a
father who had been behind them.

Young Giovanni, my precious Jean-Pierre, would always have a special place in my heart, much as I loved

the others also. I had tried to hide my favoritism, and the rest of the children did not know that Jean-Pierre was not Giovanni's son. I had argued with myself about telling him the truth many times; but I had felt that if Jean-Pierre knew that Giovanni was not his real father, he would have no sense of obligation to him, and he would leave; and I could not bear to be parted from this only remaining link with my short time of happiness.

But he was so different from the others, that people must have wondered about him. He was small, with jet black hair, and a clever and intelligent-looking face. He was so like Pierre when I first fell in love with him, that sometimes I caught my breath, and had to turn away quickly to hide my emotion. Jean-Pierre loved to read and to study. How often I had longed that he could have gone on to college, but in those days, that was almost impossible for a boy from a large poverty-stricken family like ours. Now there are grants and scholarships, but in Italy before the war, it was out of the question; anyway, Giovanni would never have allowed it. He never lost an opportunity of reminding me that Jean-Pierre was not his son, and of what I owed to him, and I did not dare suggest more for Jean-Pierre than for the rest of the family.

He was so good at languages that he could speak German and French with me, and he had even studied English with me when he had time. Maybe this aptitude would prove useful in the future.

Giovanni had no patience with his studious ways, and insisted that he learn carpentry, and so pay back some of the debt he owed to him. Jean-Pierre worked with a resigned submission, which often tore at my heart.

Romano was like Carlo, his father, a dark, easygoing boy with a happy disposition, who accepted life as he found it, and slid out of problems with amazing ease. All these years that he and Eleanora had been in school, we had drawn a small pension for them, so they owed Giovanni nothing; and to me, they were as dear as my own children; in fact, I often forgot that they were not mine by birth.

Eleanora was married when she was eighteen, and went to live in Rome; so our family was decreasing rapidly.

Ernst was the odd one among the boys. It was hard to imagine that he had Italian blood in his veins. He was all Müller, and constantly reminded me of Uncle Ernst, but he had a much more determined nature. I felt that nobody, man or woman, would wear down Ernst, as Aunt Rita had done her husband. He was tall and straight, with fair hair and blue eyes like mine, and naturally stood out among all the dark-haired and dark-eyed Italians. He was the only one whom Giovanni had never been able to subdue; and I believe that secretly, Giovanni had admired him for it. Before Ernst had grown so tall and strong, Giovanni had beaten him constantly; but Ernst would continue to go his own way, and at length his father had realized that he had met his match; and only when he was intoxicated did he ever try to pit himself against Ernst.

Then there were times when Ernst showed him very definitely who was the master. He had refused to work for Giovanni, and had obtained work in a factory. Giovanni thought he had a perfect right to every penny the boys earned, but Ernst saw that none of his wages reached his father's hands. He gave me what he could afford; then he left the rest in a savings club where he worked. There was a lot of Swiss thriftiness in Ernst's makeup. He was a hard worker, and determined to get out of the sort of life we had. He had confided to me once that someday he was determined he would go to Switzerland and make a home for me there.

For a time the boys were stationed in the neighborhood, and came home frequently. Our eldest daughter, Julie, who was seventeen, took care of the younger children while I was at work; and I felt happier than I had been for many, many years. We had escaped from the terrible bondage Giovanni had imposed upon us. I was so proud to see my boys free from the constant arguing and drunkenness. I was earning a good wage, so I could buy food and clothes for the little ones; and above all, I enjoyed my work.

What a relief it was to be away from the awful drudgery and misery. No medicine could have been so beneficial. I was able to help other people, I had contact with educated adults, and I could start to live again. I had come out of a dark prison, and could breathe freely. I had to work hard to keep up with all the duties of home, as well as put in my eight hours a day at the office, but it was like heaven after all those dark years.

Our office was a fascist organization, but it had nothing to do with politics. Our work was to give counsel and assistance to anyone who approached us; we tried to see that the right person got the right job, and we endeavored to protect the rights of such workers.

# 12

---

I DECIDED that at the first opportunity, I must tell Jean-Pierre the story of his birth; but I shrank from doing it and kept putting it off, until he arrived home one day to say that he was being sent to the French front. What a terrible sound that had for me. Was history to be repeated? The French frontier had robbed me of Pierre; was it to take Jean-Pierre from me also? I knew then that I must tell Jean-Pierre the truth; so I asked him to meet me when I left the office, and I told Julie I would be home late.

When Jean-Pierre saw me, I must have looked paler than usual for he said, "Mamma, you look ill. Are you

sure it is not too much for you to work all day, and have
so much to do at home also?"

I shook my head. "Can we go somewhere, where we
can talk without being overheard?" I asked. I knew that
it was going to take every ounce of restraint I possessed
to get through what I had to do.

"There is the park, or we can go to a restaurant," he
said.

"The park will be best. It's still very warm."

"But you will need something to eat."

"Yes, later, but first I must talk."

Evidently puzzled, Jean-Pierre took my arm, and
without speaking, we entered the park and found an un-
occupied seat in the shelter of some bushes. There were
very few people about at this time of day, so we would
not be interrupted.

"Now what dark and deathly secret do you have to
disclose?" he asked.

I started, and for a moment could not speak.

"It has been a secret for twenty years," I said quietly.
"Do you realize that your name is not Giovanni, and
that my husband is not your father?"

He went pale, and turned to stare at me. "Then who
am I?"

"The name your real father chose for you was Jean-
Pierre, but that would have been so noticeable in Italy,
that we decided to call you Giovanni. Let me tell my
story quickly; then you can question me later. I must get
it over with as soon as I can."

He nodded but did not speak.

So very quietly I told him my pathetic little story.
How I had lost my parents, and had been forced to
leave my guardian's house and Marie's home, and had
sought refuge with Pierre. I told him how kind he was to
me, and what had happened because Pierre was a foreigner. Then I told him about the day he was born, how
I waited and waited for Pierre to get in touch with me,
until finally I heard that he was dead. I told of working
in the hospital and at Dr. Demmer's, so that I could
keep him with me until I was so ill and could not go on;

then how Uncle Ernst's offer had come as an answer to prayer, and with such high hopes I had come to Italy. I had no need to go into detail concerning Aunt Rita and her family; he remembered that household too vividly himself. I described Giovanni when he came home from the army and offered to adopt Jean-Pierre as his own son, but how quickly I had regretted my promise to be engaged; then how he had come home so badly injured that he had thought he was going to die, and he had insisted that he would not undergo the necessary operation if I did not marry him first. I described how Giulia and Carlo had died, and Giulia had made me promise to take Eleanora and Romano as my own.

I told him that for the first two years we had been happy enough, until Giovanni got entangled with his family again, and started to drink heavily. There was no need to go on any further. Jean-Pierre knew only too well what sort of home life we had endured all the time he was growing up.

I ceased speaking, and my limbs were shaking. I dared not look at Jean-Pierre's face, in case I saw anger written on it. Would he forgive me for giving him such a poor start in life?

Suddenly he put his arm around my shoulders, and held me close. I turned to look at him, and his eyes were shining; then the tears of relief started pouring down my face.

"Don't cry, Mamma," he said gently. "You have no idea what this means to me. All my life I have felt that I did not belong. I could not understand it, but I never fitted in. I hated and despised my father—no, my stepfather—but I thought it was wicked to think of him in this way. I was ashamed that I belonged to him, and often I wondered how you, who are so different in every possible way, could have lowered yourself to marry such a man. Mamma mia, you have suffered so much. To have been loved by such a man as my real father, to lose him so tragically, and to be left with me to care for, then to have to endure a life like this for so many years; it is beyond thinking about.

"Now I understand so much which has puzzled me. I feel like a different person. Thank you, Mamma, for telling me this. I know how it must have hurt you to remember, but I can go away with my head held higher, because I know that fine blood flows through my veins. I will make you proud of me, Mamma. I will show you that I am a son that my father would have been proud to claim. And Mamma, I swear to you that when I come back from the war, I will take you away. Ernst has always said he will leave Italy and go to Switzerland; together we will do this for you. May I tell Ernst about it? We have shared so many secrets, even though we are so different. He is not like his father; there is strength in him. He is like you, Mamma, and will not be beaten."

"God has given me three wonderful sons," I said brokenly. "For Romano is very dear to me also."

"May I tell Ernst?" he persisted.

"Yes, if you wish, but make him promise to tell no one else. I do not want the girls to know our secret. To them you are their brother, and I am foolish enough to want to keep my happy memories to myself."

"Dear Mamma, you have been so good to us all. We can leave you with more contented minds, now that you have escaped from Papa's domination. We are so proud of what you have done, and what you are doing. Whatever happens, remember we love you with all our hearts."

We made our way back home, and pleading a blinding headache, I went to my room to lie down. This was so unusual that the children became alarmed, but Jean-Pierre understood, and offered to take them out to a movie as a last treat.

Julie brought me coffee and a little supper, and for once I indulged in the luxury of allowing my memory to go back and dwell on those short months when Pierre and I had been so happy. I felt drained and exhausted after revealing so much to Jean-Pierre, but how glad I was that there were no more secrets between us. I could send him away proud of his real father, not with a sense of disgust every time he had thought of the one who was supposed to have taken his father's place.

The next day, Jean-Pierre left; and for many days, I could scarcely bear to think of him. I worked until I was absolutely exhausted, but anything was better than dwelling on the possibility that I might never see him again.

A month later, Romano and Ernst were both sent to Africa; so I had much to pray for when I could slip into church. All around, young men were leaving for the various fronts; and then news came back of first one, and then another being killed, wounded, or taken prisoner. How long would it be before we too received one of those fateful telegrams?

The months went by, and Jean-Pierre came home for leave. He looked older and more serious, but he was proud that already he had been made a sergeant. There was even talk that he might become an officer. How proud I was. My son was being recognized, and treated as someone with intelligence and authority.

I dreamed then of what could happen when Jean-Pierre came out of the army. Perhaps he would be able to go on with his education. He would never again come back to be under Giovanni's domination, and he would be free to forge ahead in his own way. How wonderful if, in time, we could leave Italy and go as Jean-Pierre and Ernst planned, to my beloved Switzerland. We would take the younger children with us; and Giovanni could go on living in the way of his choice, which had never been mine.

Even now he was as impossible to live with as ever. He resented my freedom, resented the fact that I had money of my own to spend. He was madly jealous because people told him how much good I was doing, and how excellent I was at my job. He would use the slightest excuse to beat me and knock me about. Once I would have been ashamed to go out with bruises and black eyes. Now I did not care. It was obvious that I had gone up in people's estimation, and that they recognized my husband for what he was—a drunken bully.

So the months of war restrictions, sorrow, and uncertainty went on. Romano was wounded and came back to Italy and spent several weeks in a hospital. Ernst was captured, and later sent to Texas as a prisoner of war.

Then came the awful news that Jean-Pierre had been killed.

It was as if some living part of me had gone. I knew then that all these years, Jean-Pierre had meant more to me than everybody else in the world put together. He was all I had left of the man who had awakened me to my first and only real love. For weeks I felt numb with shock, and perhaps the hardest of all to bear, was that I could share my real grief with nobody else. Giovanni showed whatever sorrow he felt by drinking all day, and his so-called friends showed their sympathy by seeing that he was never completely sober.

If I had not had my work to go to, I do not think I could have carried on, but others were in trouble beside myself; there was untold hardship for thousands, and the best cure for my grief was to do all in my power to help them.

Night after night I found I could not sleep. Thoughts of Pierre and Jean-Pierre were always with me, and it was actual torture to have to endure the horror of sharing my bed with my senseless husband, who reeked of drink and smoke.

I tried to pray, but I felt that my words never went higher than the ceiling. I went to church to say masses, lit candles, and to pray for the soul of Jean-Pierre; but I had no assurance that any of this meant anything. I sorrowed, as one who had no hope in Christ.

Often I wondered, as I had asked Dr. Margaret years before, Is there a God who knows anything about what goes on down here, and if there is, why does He let all this wickedness and slaughter and the awful waste of human life take place?

My faith was dead. To me, God was a myth built up by the church to mislead people and retain power over them. He meant nothing to me anymore.

Julie married and moved away; but by that time, Yvonne was in school, so we managed to do the necessary housework between us. Maria and Margarita started nurse's training in a hospital, and only came home on their free days; so that left only the four younger girls. Lisa, Anna, and Renée were responsible children, quite capable of caring for Yvonne until I came home in the evenings. It seemed that our family had shrunk so suddenly that often the table looked large and empty, and the house deserted. The girls were quiet and subdued, for their father never spared them; and like myself, they were used to his beatings.

Yvonne, the baby, was the only one who was not afraid of him, and she would coax him into a better frame of mind when he was sober. When he was intoxicated, she, like the rest, had learned to keep out of his way.

She was a small, dark, vivacious child, always happy and continually singing and dancing. She was so full of fun and such a clever mimic, that we called her "Cita," the little clown. How I had hated her coming, but now I was glad of her company, and her lighthearted happiness livened up the depleted household.

I was determined that Yvonne would have a better life than the others. I would be able to dress her differently and give her a better education. Even as a child, she took dancing lessons and played the piano, and had a natural gift for both. We were all very fond of her; and if she had not been so sweet and lovable, we would have spoiled her.

One morning in 1943, when I was going to work, I noticed that crowds had gathered in several places. They were gesticulating wildly and looking very upset. Obviously, whatever had happened was not good news.

Then I saw a large poster which stated that by order of the king, General Badoglio would take over the responsibilities of the Italian government. The fascist party was dissolved, and order would be established by the regular Italian army. Everyone was ordered to go home and await developments.

I had almost reached my office, and many other employees were also converging on it. Two guards stood before the building, asking to see our identification cards and what work we did. Then we were allowed to pass. It was obvious that our office had been searched. The portraits of Mussolini had been removed from the walls, the files and documents inspected.

I started to go on with the work I had begun the previous day; but before long, an Italian colonel came in, and looked around with a set, grim face; he snapped several questions at me, then left again.

Later we learned that Mussolini had been arrested, and taken to a prearranged place, where he was to be handed over to the Anglo-American forces.

All fascist-political centers were closed, though the public assistance organizations went on as before. We had no interference in our office, but everyone was uncertain how long we would go unmolested.

Then one morning as I was taking some documents to another office, a clerk dashed out, nearly knocking me down in his excitement. He was laughing and crying, and speaking so incoherently that I thought he had taken leave of his senses.

At length I made out, "He is free, he is free again, now everything will be put right. Thank God there is still hope for our country."

"What do you mean?" I demanded. "Who is free?"

"I just heard it on the radio," he said, and tore out of the door before I could get any sense out of him.

Not until noon did we know what had happened. Mussolini had been freed from his confinement by a daring German officer.

A few days later, an armed division of German troops entered the city, stating that they had come to protect Italy from civil war; and it could well have come to that, because the whole country was in a state of turmoil and uncertainty.

Immediately all who could, tried to escape into hiding. Men let themselves down from windows with ropes made from sheets; others crawled through sewer pipes, which passed under the walls and into the outside fields, where women and children waited for them with clothes and what food and money they had hastily gathered together. Some were hidden in attics or cellars, even in the huts of horses and pigs. Anything was considered better than falling into the hands of the Germans or the fascists, and being sent to forced labor camps.

Even soldiers who were in military hospitals, escaped and tried to make their way home by whatever means they could find. Some succeeded; but others were captured and taken to the barracks, one half of which was a fascist camp, the other half German.

A few days after the German troops entered our city, I was leaving for work one morning, when I saw a woman sitting on a doorstep. The tears poured down her face as she told those who stopped to listen, that her son, who had been very ill in the military hospital of Verona, had escaped and was on the train on his way home, when the fascists had caught him and taken him back to camp. He had been able to notify her where he was; and for two days she had tried to speak to the officer in charge of the camp, but could not obtain a hearing.

She showed me her son's letter, and I decided that I would try to help her. I knew already that the man who had been principal of the school my children had attended, was now the officer in charge of the camp where this young man had been taken.

I sent a message to my office, then accompanied this woman to the camp. I knew the officer was an understanding man, and I felt sure that he would help this woman if he could.

At the camp gates, a sentry demanded to see our passes. The woman had her identity card; I had the one showing the office where I was employed. We had to leave our passes with the guard. Then we were allowed to enter, and a guard pointed out Captain Sotoni's office. Another guard phoned, asking if he would receive us, and we were taken to him. He recognized me immediately and asked what had brought me there.

I explained the case, showing him the son's letter, but

he shook his head saying, "I am afraid you're too late. If you had come yesterday, I could have handed the boy over to you, but unfortunately all the prisoners were handed over to the Germans last night, and there is nothing I can do about it." He stopped, then looked at me searchingly for a moment. "If I remember rightly, you speak German, do you not, Signora Müller? Why not try to see the German colonel himself? He is a reasonable man; perhaps he will be able to free the soldier you are looking for. Tell him that I have sent you to him, and that I would have handed over the boy if he were still here."

I thanked Captain Sotoni for his consideration, and set out to find the German in question. We had to walk the entire length of the camp, for the German colonel had his office at the opposite end. I asked the sentry on guard if I could speak to Colonel Weigand, and he took us into a waiting room.

I was taken into the colonel's office, but my companion was told to wait outside.

First I told him in German why I had come, and asked if it would be possible for the mother to see her son. He said this could be arranged. I repeated what Captain Sotoni had told me, but he also said it was too late. All the rounded-up Italian soldiers were to be shipped to Germany the following morning; copies of their names had already been sent to every town where the convoy would make a halt, and questions would be asked if any were missing.

Then I appealed to him as a father. This boy was ill with lung sickness; he had been severely wounded, and would be of no use to anybody. If he ever reached a German factory, he would die there; but if he would give him back to his mother, she could nurse him back to health. If he had a son of his own, surely this was what he would want done for him.

He answered that he was a father, but first of all he was a soldier who was under orders. He hated war and all it entailed, but he had no choice but to obey.

"I would like to grant you this favor, Signora," he

went on, "but I also have superior officers, and without their permission, I cannot sign a pass to allow this man to return to his home. If I did, my own career would be jeopardized."

*I must make one more attempt to move him,* I thought, and in a last desperate appeal, I said, "I myself do not know this boy; but if you wish to win the friendship of the Italians, you must help them."

"I will have the soldier in question sent to you," he said brusquely, and I felt myself dismissed.

As I turned to the door, he added, "If you succeed in getting this boy out of camp, I promise you that I personally will take no steps to have him recaptured."

I felt he was trying to convey some sort of message, but for the moment, I could not understand what he meant. I thanked him and went back to the waiting room. After some minutes, Signora Bindella ran forward to greet her son; and I moved into the corridor so that they could talk in private.

Up and down the corridor between the waiting room and the commander's office, an armed sentry paraded, his heavy boots clumping on the cement floor.

Suddenly I noticed that the door of the colonel's office was opening slowly. Then he came out and looked at the guard's retreating back. Suddenly he made a sign to me, which I believed meant, "Get out." I could hardly believe it, but again he made an impatient sign; and I grasped the woman and her son by the hand, whispering, "Come this way." Before the guard had turned, we were out of the building, but we were still in the camp.

I told them to walk naturally; otherwise if anyone had the idea that the boy was trying to make an escape, we could be shot. We were almost through the camp, when a voice called loudly, *"Gnädig* Frau." My legs refused to move, and I was afraid to turn around.

When I did, the German colonel I had interviewed was waving a sheet of paper at me. He must have realized the shock he had given me, for he took my arm firmly, saying, "Come with me, all of you. Do not return to the guard at the gate for your identification papers, but return for them later and come alone."

I had completely overlooked the fact that our two identification cards had been left at the gate, whereas now three people were trying to go out.

By another exit, the officer accompanied us out of the camp, and walked with us to the nearest bus stop. I took the mother and son, who were still too bewildered to take in what had actually happened, to the railway station, and saw them board a train for their hometown. In the afternoon I went back to the camp for the identification cards, explaining that we had forgotten them on the way out; and as it was a new sentry on duty, he did not ask any questions.

I sent the woman's card to the address she had given me; and when she replied, she thanked me profusely for all I had done, and told me that they had arrived home without any further trouble, and that now her son was much better and was going to an uncle in the country, where he would be safe.

This was the beginning of a new sort of work for me, which was to lead me into many dangerous and difficult problems. My knowledge of four languages opened many doors, and often I found that by appealing to a man's better nature and reminding him of his own mother or family, even the hardest was willing to assist me if he could.

One day in October 1943, an acquaintance, who was a teacher, came seeking my help for two of her relatives whose sons, together with their company of Alpini (an army troop, located in the mountains), had been trapped at Bardonnecchia at the French border by the chaotic conditions following the occupation of Italy by the German army. Everywhere in northern Italy our soldiers who were on active service tried to escape being drafted into the German army, and so sent to the distant fighting fronts, or to labor camps.

Many succeeded, for almost every house was open to them, where they would be supplied with civilian clothes, food, and hospitality as long as they needed to stay. Germany might be an ally; but Italians had no love for Hitler, or for being sent to foreign units to fight Hitler's wars.

Many from southern Italy could not reach their own homes, so they had to stay in hiding, or try to cross the mountains to get away from the danger of capture by the Nazis.

I arranged with Lisa that I might be away for one or two nights; the children were older now, and not so dependent on me; and I had ceased to care very much about what my husband did or said.

There was only one train a day crossing northern Italy from Venice to the French border. Signora Donelli and Signora Antoni and I were forced to spend the night in the Milan station, which had been bombed just a few days previously. There were no lights anywhere, but the full moon shone down on a heartbreaking scene. We had no roof over us, as it had been destroyed. Hundreds of refugees tried to sleep on the cement floor, which was covered with rubble and debris; their pathetic little bundles of possessions under their heads for pillows, and what rags they had, pulled closely around them. Babies cried, people groaned; and for me at least, sleep was impossible.

By six o'clock the next morning when the train for Turin was ready to leave, it was packed to capacity, with many other would-be travelers clinging to the outside supports, until the railway officials forced them to get down.

As we traveled, terrible scenes of desolation met our eyes, especially as we neared Turin, which had suffered severe bombing raids.

Later in the afternoon, we climbed aboard the train to the border through the Susa valley. On our left, the setting sun lit up the countryside as if to hide much of the devastation; and on our right, beyond the valley, were the mountains of southern Switzerland. My eyes filled, and my heart ached to see again the beauty of my own country. What ever evil puny man brought upon the world, creation stood unchanged. When all this misery and slaughter was over, its majesty would still remain.

It was dark when we arrived at Bardonnecchia, and we had difficulty finding a place to sleep. At length we found a small hotel, where we had supper and went to bed.

The next morning, as we were coming downstairs, we met a young German officer. My companions could not speak German; in fact, that is why they had asked me to accompany them.

He greeted us pleasantly, and I replied in his own tongue. He looked surprised as I went on to inquire where I could find the Platzkommandant. He offered to take me to him, remarking what a pleasure it was to listen to his mother tongue spoken by a woman. I believed he was homesick, and thought of my sons who must have often felt the same.

He inquired why I had come to this lonely, out-of-the-way place, and I explained the reason. He took us to the Platzkommandant and introduced me. The commander asked for the names of the two men we were seeking, gave the officer a list with the names of all Italian soldiers under their command, wished me good luck, and promised to give me a release certificate as soon as we could find the men we wanted.

Still accompanied by the young officer, we went to a dynamited tunnel where many Italian and German soldiers were working, but Giorgio Donelli and Bruno Antoni were not there. Then an Italian soldier informed us that both the men we were looking for had been chosen that morning to go to France with a group of Italian and German soldiers, to take food supplies to a German camp on the other side of the mountain. It would be three or four days until they returned; so if we wished to contact them, we would have to wait.

I thought about my family; but having come so far, I could not leave these women here on their own. We went back to the hotel where we had spent the night, all of us tired and anxious. It was very cold, and it was raining. The whole place made us feel utterly depressed. In the evening of our third day of waiting, the young German officer who had previously helped us, came to our table. He looked worried, and I immediately sensed that something had gone wrong.

"We do not know all the details," he said hurriedly in German, "but we have learned that the group we sent to France has not arrived there. We believe that the Italians attacked the guards, killed them, and then fled into the mountains. If this is what has happened, you must leave immediately."

I thanked him and promised to leave with my companions as soon as we could get a train. I gave him the address of my office in Verona, in case there was any news which would help.

I told Signora Donelli and Signora Antoni that there had been trouble between the Germans and Italians, and it was unsafe for us to wait any longer. I did not tell them what the German officer suspected, so that they had no idea that their sons were on the run.

We had to wait at the station for five hours for the train to start. There were armed German guards everywhere, and our train was inspected every few minutes while it stood there. Obviously they believed that the wanted men would try to board the train.

At last the signal for departure was given, and thankfully I took my companions away from Bardonnecchia. They were very disappointed, but I could not tell them the real reason for our hurried departure.

As I was looking out of the window, feasting on the beauty of the autumn colors, I noticed a movement among the trees; then I saw an Italian soldier in a tattered uniform trying to keep pace with the train. Obgiously he hoped to jump on and cling to the outside handles or buffers.

I opened my window and made signs for him to climb into our car, which was the last. The train was climbing, so was not traveling very fast, and we managed to open the door sufficiently for him to climb in. He collapsed on the floor, panting, a wreck of a human being, unshaven and filthy, with rags round his feet instead of boots. He stared around at us like a hunted animal. No one in the carriage spoke a word at first; then one woman got up and offered him her seat. Another offered him some food from her bag, and he ate it ravenously. Signora Donelli reached for her suitcase, and from it took a long civilian coat she had brought for her son; while Signora Antoni took off her black shawl and wrapped it around his head to hide his ragged beard. We pushed him into the seat next to the window. He was very thin; so with these two plump women dressed in their voluminous garmets, he could hardly be seen.

It was almost uncanny that Italian women, who are usually so garrulous, could act so silently and with one accord, without being told.

I whispered to him not to move if a guard came into our car, then all of us started talking rapidly in Italian about anything that came into our heads—except the German occupation.

When the train stopped at the next station, I put my head out of the window, and saw some German guards enter the first car. Ours was the fourth and last, so I had a few moments to decide what to do.

I went to our door, and the instant the guards came in the corridor, I went toward them and greeted them in German. *Grüss Gott, meine Kinder,*" I said, as if I were delighted to see them. They were so surprised that they started to talk pleasantly enough, but evidently saw nothing beyond a collection of large Italian women talking together.

I edged them toward the exit door, talking all the time, and bid them a gay "*Auf Wiedersehen,*" when I saw them jump down from the train.

I went back to my seat, my legs trembling under me. As the train started once more, the boy reached over and grasped my hands. There were tears in his eyes as he said, "A thousand, thousand thanks, Signora."

We reached Turin where the boy lived, without further trouble. As we continued on our journey, we laughed as we thought of how we had duped the guards; and we talked of how excited the boys mother would be when he walked into his home.

Signora Donelli and Signora Antoni wept a little, because their sons were not coming home with them; but I cheered them by saying that as we had helped the unknown young man, so some other Italian mothers would help their sons to escape. (Three months later I had news that both sons had reached home after a terrible journey over the mountain passes.)

When I got home that night, I was drained and exhausted. Only then did I realize how much the continued strain had taken out of me. But tiredness was soon forgotten, when I found Romano waiting for me. He put his arms around me, and tears ran down my cheeks. How wonderful it was to have even one of my boys safely back home. The children gave me a great welcome, and we were happy for a little while.

"Papa is angry because you have been away longer than we expected," Lisa informed me, when I asked where he was. "Of course he is off to the usual place. He hasn't come any night until long after we were all in bed." She tossed her head angrily. She had no patience with her father, and there were frequent rows between them. Lisa had developed into a very independent young lady; and if the rest of us were afraid of Giovanni's violent outbursts, she wasn't. Sometimes I wondered if it would be better to let her move away from home, because I was afraid that one day, he would do her serious damage.

I told them about our journey and what had happened at the camp.

"Romano, if you stay here, aren't you likely to be rounded up with the rest and sent to Germany, or to one of the other battlefronts?" I asked.

Romano smiled. "I don't intend to give them the chance, Mamma mia. I had to come home to see you and the girls, but I'm not wandering around the streets. I'll collect what money the Italian army owes me, then I'm making my way back to Ethiopia. I liked that country, and I believe there's money to be made there. One of my friends has bought land by the side of a lake, very cheaply. He wants me to go into partnership with him, and plant fruit gardens  Labor is cheap, and the climate is good  I'm not coming back to let Papa treat me as he did before."

I looked at Romano, and I realized that perhaps I would never see him again; he was a man now, and independent, and I was glad that he was ambitious enough to make a new life for himself.

"Will you be able to see Eleanora?" I asked.

"I have already visited her, but I would not let her tell you, in case I never got this far. She has two fine children, Mamma, and she told me to say that she is trying to keep her house and family as you taught her."

"And what about yourself?" I asked. "Don't you ever think of marriage?"

He laughed. "I have asked Marie Biani to wait for me until I can make money and buy a home for her, and she has promised."

"She is a fine girl," I said in relief. I was glad that Romano would have an Italian girl to share this strange new life.

"Now I think we will go to bed," I suggested. "I am very tired, and I must be at the office early tomorrow."

"Sleep in my room tonight; then Papa will not disturb you when he comes in," Lisa suggested.

"Very well," I answered, for I dreaded what would happen if Giovanni came in fighting drunk.

"I promised I would see Marie again tonight, when few people are on the street," Romano said, and picked up his cap.

*What a handsome boy he is,* I thought. How proud Giulia and Carlo would be if they could see him.

About an hour later, I heard Giovanni stumble in the front door. He probably saw my handbag on the table and guessed I was back, for he tramped upstairs, threw open the door of my own bedroom, then bellowed, "Annalisa, where are you?"

"Lie still, Mamma, I will speak to him," Lisa, who had not undressed, commanded; but I had already started to pull on some clothes.

Lisa went out, pulling her bedroom door behind her.

"Mamma is back but is very tired," I heard her say calmly. "Go to bed; you can talk to her in the morning, Papa."

"Get out of the way, girl," he yelled, and must have pushed her, for I heard her thud against the wall.

The door flew open, and Giovanni staggered in, his face red, his hair on end, and his eyes bloodshot.

*What a revolting sight,* flashed through my mind.

"So my lady wife has deigned to return," he stormed. "What sort of a wife have I got, who goes off without even telling her husband where she's going? I'll see that she knows who's boss here."

He lunged at me, grabbed my hair, and began to pound my head on the wall; but at that moment a pair of arms reached out and grasped him round the neck.

He let me go, and with a roar, turned on the new assailant; but Romano was too quick for him, and as his fist met Giovanni's chin, he staggered, fell over a chair, and went down with a crash.

The children, aroused by the noise, screamed; and I stepped over Giovanni's body to get them out of the way.

"Lisa," I called, "keep the children in their rooms," but Lisa was not there.

I looked behind me and saw Giovanni with murder in his eyes, trying to rise to his feet.

"I'll kill you for that," he shouted. "This is what I get for bringing up other people's brats. I'll kill you and that cursed woman who calls herself my wife."

"No, you won't," another voice said from the doorway. Giovanni sat down heavily on the side of the bed, all the bravado oozing out of him.

"What are you doing in my house?" he demanded, trying to bluster.

"Come to take you to the station for the night, so that you can calm down," the police marshal informed him, and slipped some handcuffs on his wrists.

"I haven't done anything," Giovanni whimpered.

"You are drunk. You threatened to kill your wife and your son, so the judge will have something to say about that. Have you forgotten that you were ordered to allow your wife to work unmolested? She is doing important work for our country. You ought to be proud of her, instead of beating her up."

"Don't arrest him, officer," I begged. "He will have forgotten in the morning."

"I must do my duty," the young marshal said sternly. "You are a disgrace to our town, Giovanni Müller. Everyone knows what a drunken bully you are; yet you have a good wife and a fine family."

"Give him another chance," I persisted.

"Will you promise never to beat your wife again?" he demanded.

"She isn't fit to be my wife. All she wants is to go away and leave her husband and children."

"Don't talk nonsense. No other woman would have put up with you all these years as she has done. Now she could have you punished, yet here she is begging me not to arrest you. You ought to have a stretch in prison to let you realize what a fool you are. I may even get into trouble myself for this; but I'll let you off this last time, if you promise you'll never strike or threaten your wife again."

Giovanni glared from one to the other, then said, "Take these cursed things off. She isn't worth going to prison for."

The young marshal slowly and deliberately removed the handcuffs, pulled Giovanni to his feet, and propelled him to the door. "Bed is the best place for you," he said, "but I'll be around to see there is no more disturbance."

Giovanni cursed us all violently, then banged his bedroom door. I could imagine so vividly how he would throw himself on the bed fully dressed, even to his filthy boots, and before a few moments, be snoring loudly.

The policeman laughed quietly as he rattled the cuffs.

"How did you know we needed you?" I asked.

He looked at Lisa, and her face flushed as she smiled back at him.

"Lisa told me there might be trouble, so although I'm

really off duty, I hung around until I saw her father leave the tavern.

"Lisa and I want to get married, Signora Müller. What do you think your husband will say to a policeman being in your family?"

"You'd better move in here," Romano said with a wide grin. "Then Mamma will be sure of having peace for the first time in her married life."

"Is it all right, Mamma?" Lisa demanded.

"I'm delighted," I replied, and held out my hands to them both. "I had no idea this was in the wind."

"We have known each other a long time," Paolo said. "I have wanted Lisa since she was a little girl, but I had to wait until she grew up."

"My family is decreasing very rapidly," I said rather sadly, then pulled myself up sharply, and added, "but I am proud of you all, and am so happy to see you making good homes. Margarita and Marie will be married as soon as their boyfriends return, Eleanora and Juliana have settled, now Romano is preparing to start a home in another country. There will be only four left, and I don't suppose Ernst will stay at home very long. Anna is old enough to look after the house now, so you and Paolo can make your plans without worrying about us, Lisa."

"I wish all the family could be at my wedding," Lisa said wistfully. "Especially Giovanni. It is so hard to remember he will never be with us again. He was such an extra-special brother."

"He was an extra-special person altogether," Romano added. "You know he always seemed different from the rest of us. Ernst is more unlike the other members of the family in looks, but Giovanni was sort of better than the rest of us. Too bad he had to be named after—*him*," he said, gesturing toward his father's room.

I could not speak. Was this the time for me to tell them who young Giovanni really was? No, I could not bring myself to go through that ordeal again. Besides, they had paid their tribute to him, and I wanted them to go on thinking of him as a dear and special brother, not someone divorced from their own background.

"Go to bed, Mamma," Lisa said, evidently alarmed by the palor of my face. "Papa won't wake again to-night, and when he remembers tomorrow, he'll feel very small and stupid."

"There has to be no more threatening or beating any-one up," Paolo said firmly. "Even if he is Lisa's father, I'll take him in and teach him a lesson."

"I don't know why you want to marry me with such a father," Lisa said, and my heart ached for her.

"Your mother makes up for him," Paolo said, putting his arm around her. "But remember, if you aren't a good wife, I'll beat you too," he said with a laugh, as he looked down tenderly into her glowing face.

"Then you'll have to go to prison too," she replied pertly.

"Come on, Mamma, we're not needed here," Romano said, putting his arm through mine and leading me off to bed.

"Good night, Mamma mia," he said, hugging me very close. "No real mother could have loved me better than you have done. This family owes everything to you."

As I got into bed, I could not see through my tears. All the hard work, the poverty, the misery, were noth-ing, when I knew that my children felt this way about me. No queen could have felt more honored than I did that night.

# 13

———◆———

TWO DAYS AFTER I RETURNED from Bardonnecchia, a high ranking German officer came to our office, asking for personnel for the numerous offices the Germans had opened since their arrival. They needed office clerks, interpreters, translators, and intercommunication officials.

The head of our department was not present; and as no one else could speak German, he was brought to my office. He explained why he had come and asked if I would pass on his request.

Then he asked what sort of work I did, and I told him. I had several puzzling cases concerning emigrants to Germany, so I asked if he knew to whom I should forward these and future queries. He replied that if I would give him a list of the names and addresses of the workers, together with the names of the factories which had employed them, he would be glad to make the necessary inquiries himself.

He asked me to type a note which he dictated; then after he had examined it, he said, "We are desperately in need of good translators and interpreters. If you consider changing to a much better paid position, please get in touch with me."

I thanked him for his offer, but said that I liked the sort of service which I was giving, and that I believed I was needed here.

A few days later, another German officer came to the office. He explained that he was the head of the new employment bureau for those going to Germany, and that I was being transferred to his office, because I was the only person who understood this type of work and also spoke German. I did not want this change, but I had no choice in the matter. For the moment, the Germans dictated the terms.

I had to accompany Colonel Fleishman to the city authorities, to furniture stores, supply depots, etc. I detested this man from the beginning. He was an arrogant, bullying man of the worst type.

When we went in to a store, if his requirements were not met immediately, he took out his gun, and put it on the counter with a very menacing gesture, saying that the merchant had better make sure that the merchandise he required was forthcoming, or there would be trouble. The Germans were supposed to be our allies, but there was nothing friendly about this man's attitude.

Now I hated going to work. All the joy had been taken out of my job, and I asked to have my old position back again.

"We are sorry we can do nothing about it," the director of my former employment agency replied to my request. "*They* are the bosses now, and we must obey them in every detail. God help us."

I stayed at home for a few days, saying I was sick; then the police came to see if I was really ill, so I had to return. But I felt I could not go on, so finally I sent in my resignation.

Even this had no effect. The reply came that for the duration of the war, everybody had to stay in their own jobs in order to win it. I was determined, however, that somehow I would get away from Colonel Fleishman; so I requested an interview with Colonel Schpreder, the German officer who had come to my office in the first place.

I told him that I disliked working for Colonel Fleishman, but that my office would not accept my resignation. He was very pleasant, and agreed that it was impossible for me to cease working, but that I could choose among any of the numerous German offices where translators and interpreters were needed. He offered me a long list, and when I had examined it, I chose the press. He called the press office himself, and informed them that I was being sent to work there, and called the office of Colonel Fleishman to say I was being transferred to the press.

When I arrived at the office indicated, I was given a newspaper article to translate and was accepted immediately. At first I was with a German officer who was an editor in civilian life. We had several Italian newspapers to examine. All I had to do was to read the military and political articles to him in German. One day he did not turn up, so I worked on as usual, and wrote the translation on paper. When he arrived very late in the day, he seemed surprised that I should have gone on working in his absence. He took my translation to the commander, and from then on they gave me the marked papers and let me do the rest myself. This gave me the opportunity several times of leaving out passages which could have brought trouble to the writer. Later, when several other translators joined the staff, I had to be very careful about any alterations.

Later on, the contacts I made in the press office helped me a great deal when I tried to assist people whose relatives had been arrested by the Germans, or by the fascists, or when their houses had been seized.

The Germans in the press office were educated, well-bred men, themselves writers, journalists, and editors; and I had nothing but respect and high regard for them.

I had been working for the press for some time, when I began to realize that it was impossible for me to go on living under such high pressure. I had not had a day off for many years, because when I was not at the office, there were always untold tasks to be attended to at home.

In all my twenty-four years of married life, I had never had a vacation, not even one day free from cares and problems.

Several times I found myself getting off the bus at some place I had never intended going, and I realized that my mind was having spells of blankness or black-

outs, when I did not remember anything. It was no good
appealing to Giovanni, and I did not want to make a
fuss; but I decided that I would insist on a couple of
days freedom from the office, when I could go off by
myself.

One morning I left home as usual, but instead of taking the bus to work, I took one going the opposite direction; then I walked slowly toward the hills. Some friends
of mine, an older couple, Signor and Signora Negri, had
taken refuge in a small village there. I had agreed to
send them medicines, and attend to other matters for
them. They had invited me to visit them many times, but
I had never been free to do so before.

Now I felt that the long walk in the fresh air, and the
silence, would do me good. It was a beautiful September
morning. There was the scent of hay and dried grass in
the air; the trees and plants were beginning to change to
autumn colors. How good it was to be away from the
rush and bustle of the city, to breathe the clean air and
feel the light breeze ruffling my hair.

Halfway up the hill, I sat down on a rock to enjoy the
beauty and peace all around me. I though of Giovanni,
so bound by his own foolish weaknesses; I thought of
my children, and remembered Jean-Pierre, who would
never again be able to enjoy all this beauty. He had
been so young, so full of promise; why had God taken
him from me as he had taken Pierre? For a few moments, I was overcome with bitterness. The church said
we must love God and never question His dealings with
us; it was a sin worthy of eternal perdition to doubt
God, but during the years, I had turned away from such
unrealistic dogmas. The church now meant nothing to
me. I was overcome with doubts, and found no comfort
in carrying out the empty rituals. I believed I could best
please God—if there was a God—by helping other people and doing the best I could. I felt I must work for my
salvation, not rely upon the church or the priest.

But this morning as I sat looking around on the wide
expanse, I was once more calmed in my spirit, and again
conscious of a power outside myself. I did not under-

stand, but Someone far greater than I was must have
created this majesty. Someday when I had more time, I
would search again to find the peace which Dr. Margaret had talked about so many years ago.

As it was almost noon, I decided to climb further;
then looking down the path, I saw another woman approaching, carrying a suitcase. I waited for her and we
went upward together. It did not take us long to get acquainted.

Her name was Signora Bertin. She told me she had
been to the Fascist Women's Club with clothing for the
school-children. She spoke of how little the children
had; how much many of them had suffered, owing to
the war; and that she tried to collect clothes to help
them before winter came on. Her only son was an
officer in the Italian army and had been stationed in Verona before he was sent to Africa. Now she was waiting
for the war to end and her son to come back to her.

She was a well-spoken, refined woman, who spoke
with a slight accent, as she came originally from one of
the islands off the coast. Her husband had been a colonel, but had been killed at the beginning of the war.

We walked to the village together, and I greatly enjoyed the conversation. When I arrived at the house of
the Negris, they were working in their small garden. I
thought their welcome was frigid; then as I waved farewell to Signora Bertin, Signora Negri dragged me into
the house.

"How did you come to be friendly with *that* woman?"
she demanded.

I looked at her in bewilderment. "I met her as I came
up the hill, and we walked up together. I enjoyed talking
with her very much."

Signor Negri burst out, "She is a spy, sent here to in-
form on us. Didn't you hear how she speaks?"

"But her husband was killed in our army; her son is
even now fighting in Africa!" I exclaimed.

"All lies," they burst out. "Who can prove it? Who
has heard of anyone called Bertin in these parts? She is
a German, we tell you. She pretends to care for the chil-

dren; but she gets them to talk, then she informs against the partisans."

"I'm sure you're mistaken. She seemed to me to be a pleasant, sincere lady," I replied, beginning to feel exasperated.

"She is a foreigner, an outsider; we do not want such as she among us."

"But what grounds do you have for your suspicions?"

"We have seen her with a German officer. He carried her suitcase for her."

"But that proves nothing. He probably met her accidentally like I did, and offered to carry her bag."

"You are from the city. You know nothing of what goes on in the hills," they said sneeringly. "We do not submit as you do."

I felt that I was among strangers. These were not the kindly people I had known and helped, but it was useless to argue. My day was spoiled; and as soon as I could, I bid them good-bye and made my way downhill. I did not see the lady again, and I did not try to visit the Negris after that. The road was declared unsafe for ordinary travel because of constant raids by the partisans.

We knew that most of the partisans were not patriots, as they pretended to be. Many had changed their political views several times, according to the ups and downs of war. They had been fascists, then partisans, then back to fascists. Many were criminals who had escaped from justice or deserted from the army. They were outlaws, and had no compunction about killing, if that suited their purpose.

Some years later, after the end of the war, I came across an old newspaper. In it I saw the account of a trial. An Italian officer, back from a prison camp in Algeria, had discovered that his mother, who had been living in the village of Bellavista during his absence, had been buried alive by the partisans just before the arrival of the Allied troops.

I dropped the paper, and felt physically sick. This was the lady I had met that September day in the hills, and this had been the terrible fate that an ignorant, stupid mob had wreaked on her. Then I remembered that just prior to the arrival of the Allied troops in Verona, I had met Signor Negri, my onetime friend, wearing a red ribbon around his right sleeve, to show that he was a leader of the partisans. He had been one of the murderers, for he must have known what was happening.

For days, I could not get the thought of the sufferings of that poor woman who had already given her husband to her country, out of my mind. Somehow I must try to get in touch with her son, yet what good could I do?

Again I cried, "God, are You dead? Why do the devil and his servants triumph and bring such evil into the world?"

I had returned to my job the next day, and we were as embroiled as ever in the business of survival. Although I had taken a brief respite, the war had not.

The war dragged on so long that it was hard to remember a time when we had not seen uniforms filling the streets, heard of tragedies every day, read of bombings, ships being sunk, and all the attendant horrors of war. How much longer could this awful thing continue? Reading the news each day as I did at the office, I was aware that the tide had turned for Hitler. Mussolini had been deposed; Hitler was following in his footsteps. All we longed for was peace—at any price!

One afternoon in March 1945, a lady I had never seen before, stopped me on the street and introduced herself as the wife of a general of the Italian Anti-Aircraft Corps, the headquarters of which was near my home. I knew the general by sight; in fact, Giovanni had done some carpentry work for him. She offered to give me a lift home in her car; and although I was mystified, I accepted. Once we had set off, she informed me that her husband needed an interpreter, and that she was taking me directly to their villa. I said I must go home to change, but she replied that there was no time. She explained that some days ago a certain German general had visited the Italian general's headquarters, but he did not wish to reveal the reason for his visit, through an official interpreter. He had asked for another appointment, when a private interpreter could be present.

We arrived just ahead of the two officers. The Italian general left me alone for a few moments with the German, who introduced himself very politely. After a short exchange, he said, "How is it that someone with such an excellent knowledge of the German language is not working in a German office?"

Stupidly, I fell into the trap and admitted that I was employed at the press office as a translator.

At this moment the signora announced that the dinner was served, so we moved into the dining room.

Then began one of the most interesting, but also the most exasperating conversations in which I had ever been involved.

The German general used highly diplomatic skill; and we wandered into a labyrinth of involved questions, answers, and statements. He never gave a straight answer to any of the other general's questions, or made any definite commitment himself.

I felt I was moving in a thick fog and could not see where the conversation was leading. I thought I could understand the reason. He was afraid to let *me* know what he wanted to tell the general. If only I had not let slip the information that I was employed by the Germans, he might have spoken out clearly.

Thoroughly exasperated, I said in German, "Please make clear to the general what is on your mind. I promise that I will never disclose what has taken place here tonight."

But even this did not help. The more he tried to hide the real reason for this meeting, the clearer it became that it was very dangerous for him if it became known to the German Platzkommandant.

It was very late when this unsatisfactory and frustrating affair ended. While we were descending the stairs, the German asked me if he could offer me a lift back to Lake Garda, where he was to meet some friends; then he would take me home immediately afterward.

I replied that I could not delay any longer. My family

would be anxious, and I must get home as quickly as possible.

We had reached his car, and he was trying to persuade me to get in the open door, when the Italian general grasped my arm firmly and pulled me back, saying, "My chauffeur is waiting for you. I will accompany the general."

I felt a wave of relief surge over me, for I had suddenly experienced such a sense of danger that my heart was hammering, while my body was icy cold. How thankful I was to reach my own home, poor though it was, compared with the house where I had dined that evening.

The following day, the Italian general called me to his office. The first thing he said was, "Do you realize that I saved your life last night? Why did you divulge the fact that you were working with the Germans?"

"Because I had no idea at first what this meeting was about."

"Didn't my wife explain everything to you?"

"She explained nothing, except that I was to act as an interpreter for you when a German general visited you."

"That was a mistake. I expected her to put you on your guard. However, we can do nothing now. What did you understand about the situation? What was he trying to convey?"

"I understood that he was asking you to withdraw the remaining Italian army in order to open the way for the oncoming Allied forces who have already reached the Po River. The fact that he mentioned General Clark could easily be interpreted as, 'I am in touch with him and am charged with the task of engineering a cease-fire by the Italian Anti-Aircraft Corps.' "

The general said that was what he himself had gathered, but he still had high hopes that by eliminating Mussolini, he himself could rebuild what was left of the Italian army.

I replied with as much courage as I could muster, that Italy was sick and tired of war; and the sooner it ended, the better for the whole country.

# 14

----◆----

WHEN AT LONG LAST the Allied forces entered Italy, most Italians, in their innermost hearts, welcomed them with relief. At last they would get rid of the German occupation, and our men would be able to come back home.

I was offered a job in the American Red Cross office, and how glad I was now that I had learned English, though I needed a great deal of practice in speaking the language.

As an interpreter, and having had Red Cross training, I had free entry to concentration camps and hospitals, and I loved having this work.

I enjoyed working with the Americans; they were so different from many of the Germans. They were more easy-going, and treated women with greater respect, and were kind to the children.

Ernst came home from the army an older, more mature man, who had given the seven best years of his life to his country. He had fought in Yugoslavia and France, then had been sent as a bersagliere (member of the special infantry) to Africa. He had been taken prisoner during the retreat from the border of Egypt, and sent to Algiers to a French prisoner-of-war camp. He had escaped from that after some months, but had been recaptured by the Americans, then transferred to Texas.

As he was the only son left, Giovanni insisted that he should carry on the business; but Ernst had seen a great deal of the world by this time; he was twenty-nine, and in no mood to take orders from his father.

"I'm going to Switzerland, Mamma," he said. "I have never forgotten that dream. When I've got a good business started, you will come to me and bring the girls with you."

"But you will be married and have your own family," I replied.

"Maybe if I can find a Swiss girl like you, Mamma, but she must be willing to share her home with you."

I laughed shakily. "Wait and see, my son. Someday I would love to visit you in my own beautiful country, but I would not like to hinder your marriage by having your wife share a home, as I did when I first came to Italy."

Renée, who was now eighteen years old, fell in love with Pietro, a returned war veteran. He had lost both of his arms while unscrewing a live bomb, which exploded. I felt sure that to Renée he was a romantic war hero, and that if left alone, she would soon get over her infatuation.

Giovanni, however, was furious at the very idea. He beat her and took her food away from her when she came home from work ravenously hungry. This I knew only drove her further from us.

She secretly packed her belongings and moved to Pietro's home and was married there. So one more of our family was estranged because of Giovanni's pigheadedness. Sometimes I visited Renée in secret; sometimes she met me in town; but she would not come home. She was very happy and declared that Pietro was a good husband. He needed her; and Renée had always been a softhearted child, who had lavished affection on all and sundry.

Giovanni had by this time bought a motorcycle, which was ridiculous at his age and with his intemperate habits. I begged him not to get it, and others advised against it, but in all his life he had never listened to reason; so he simply laughed and called us a bunch of sissies.

He roared around the town like a teenager, and often

I expected him to be brought home dead. He had three minor accidents, but he seemed indestructable; and some nights when he reached home safely, yet he could hardly stand up straight, I felt that the saying, "The devil looks after his own," surely applied to him. He appeared to have a charmed life, so I ceased to worry about him.

I had a good job and was not dependent on him now. Yvonne worked in the same office as I did. She was the only daughter unmarried; and if it had not been for my husband, I could have been perfectly happy.

Unfortunately, by law I was compelled to endure the torture of living with him. I decided I would sleep in Yvonne's bedroom, but this threw Giovanni into a terrible rage. He even reported me to our parish priest, who visited me and delivered a severe lecture. Giovanni was my husband; by the law of holy church I was compelled to sleep with him and obey him in every way.

"But every night he comes home the worse for drink, Father," I expostulated.

"Then it is for you to have compassion. He is a poor, failing mortal, and full of sin; but what you are suggesting is of far greater wickedness. The holy church commands you to submit to your husband, and be ever ready to fulfill the part of a wife. Otherwise, you are in danger of losing your immortal soul."

In utter disgust I consented to go back to share his bed, but my faith in the church was dead. If this was what it demanded, then I wanted no part of it.

Night after night, I lay in bed dreading the sound of the motorcycle or Giovanni's stumbling steps. How I revolted at the thought of having to sleep with this man reeking with beer, smoke, and perspiration. I loathed the feel of his hand upon me. I had to submit to his bestial lust, but I felt degraded and unclean; and often after he was snoring, I got up again, washed, and slept in another bed. Only a woman who had been made to endure this sort of nightly torture can understand the physical revulsion he aroused in me.

One day at work, I had a phone call to say my husband had met with an accident and had been taken to the hospital. I was not upset, for I had come to the conclusion that nothing serious could ever happen to him. I was convinced that I would be the first one to die.

When I reached the hospital, however, I found that this time he was in critical condition. I could not leave him, and I sat by his bedside all night, but for a long time he did not recognize me.

During the night, his voice never ceased, and few of the other patients got any sleep.

The next morning, he was a little more rational and kept saying, "Take this stuff off my chest." His ribs and collar bone were broken; and obviously there was pressure on his lungs, for his breathing was difficult.

When someone came to relieve me, I walked slowly around his bed, and I saw that his eyes were following me; then to my amazement he said, "Annalisa, forgive me. I am sorry."

I could hardly believe my ears, but two others heard the words also. For the first time in over thirty years, Giovanni had apologized.

He died that same evening.

We prayed for his soul, but we also thanked God that it was all over.

How empty and how peaceful the house was now. I was able to go to bed and sleep in peace; and I was not lonely, for I had Yvonne, and others of the family often visited us. Renée, now that her father was dead, came home with her disabled husband, and Lisa came with her policeman husband and their baby.

In our town, the southern European Allied forces had their headquarters, and many Americans were stationed there. One Christmas Eve, Yvonne invited an American GI named Andy to spend Christmas with us. All the family who were within traveling distance joined us, either sleeping in the house, or coming for the day; and that Christmas we were very happy. The war was behind us; Romano was prospering in Ethiopia, Ernst in Switzerland; Juliana could not come from Rome, as another baby was expected; but Maria, Margarita, Lisa, Anna,

and Renée with their husbands and families, filled the
house to overflowing; and my heart was full as I looked
at them.

I had so much to be thankful for, and I had every
right to be proud of my family. I could not honestly say
that I was sorry my husband was not there, for he had
never contributed to our happiness. I thought of Jean-
Pierre, and when the girls went to church, I reminded
them to buy candles and say special prayers for his soul,
but somehow I did not feel so depressed. In some subtle
way I felt Pierre and Jean-Pierre were near me.

Since Giovanni's death, I had tried to put the years of
misery behind me, and so often it seemed that the
months of my happiness with Pierre were more real than
all that had gone in between.

We enjoyed having Andy with us, and from that night
he became a frequent visitor. It was evident that he was
attracted to Yvonne. He was a tall, fair-haired young
man with a beguiling manner, and he and Yvonne appeared well matched, for both of them were easygoing
and lighthearted.

We liked him, and believed he would make Yvonne
happy, although I dreaded the thought of her going off
to the other side of the world. I wrote to his mother, and
heard about his home and family, and thought everything was aboveboard. Fifteen months after that Christmas Eve, Andy and Yvonne were married, and set off
for their new life in the United States.

Yvonne wrote frequently, telling me about the people
she had come to live among and their strange customs.
At first her letters had bubbled over with joy, but gradually I noted that some of the glow had worn off, and
there were less frequent references to her husband. I
was puzzled and mystified, because almost every time I
received a letter, Yvonne was using a different address.
There was no mention of Andy, and I sensed that things
were not as they should be. I wrote to his mother, but got
no reply; so I tried his sister, and she wrote telling me
the truth.

She told me that once, before the war, Andy had had

a girl friend, but when she told him she was pregnant, he refused all responsibility, and had disappeared, and they had not heard from him again until he was abroad in the army. When Yvonne told him that she was going to have a baby, he insisted that she have an abortion and get rid of the child, as he did not want to be saddled with a family. Yvonne refused, and Andy simply walked out on her and went away with a woman who had already been divorced. His sister said that Yvonne knew that Andy had been unfaithful to her many times since they came to America, and that life had not been easy for her. Now she had a job as a housekeeper to a friend who ran a store, and was managing to support herself.

I learned all this just a few days before Yvonne wrote to tell me that her baby had been born.

I was almost frantic at the thought of my lighthearted happy Yvonne alone in a strange land. All the memories of what I had suffered after I had lost Pierre came back to haunt me, and I could not sleep or concentrate on anything else.

I wrote, asking Yvonne to bring her baby home, but she replied that she would not come back to let people talk about her. She had been so proud of her handsome American, but how people would scoff when they knew what a travesty her marriage had proved.

I decided then that if Yvonne could not come to me, I would go to her. I could not endure the thought of the struggle she would have, to work and care for her little one alone.

The rest of the family did not oppose me; in fact, they tried to help, and between us we gathered the money for my flight ticket. I visited each of my children, because I had no idea how long it would be before I saw them again. Then I went to Switzerland to say farewell to Ernst. He had a good position, and was engaged to a very fine Swiss girl, and I left him satisfied concerning his future.

How glad I was, as I set off on my long flight, that I had learned English. I had never flown before, and my heart was beating rapidly as I boarded the plane for

Amsterdam. I had been told that there was very little to
be seen from a plane, as it is above the clouds most of
the time, and that it is best to try to sleep on a long trip;
but I was afraid to miss anything, and kept my eyes
glued on the window.

At Amsterdam I was told that there had been a mistake on my ticket. No plane left for Vancouver, Canada,
until three o'clock the next day. I was taken to the Park
Hotel, and had my first sight of the Dutch city we had
heard of so often during the war. I had supper and went
to bed, but I could not sleep. I kept thinking of Yvonne,
who with her baby, would be waiting for me at San
Francisco.

How excited I was to see the snow and ice as we flew
over the Arctic Circle. I even took a photograph of an
enormous iceberg shining like gold in the sun. The sun
had been in front of us for nineteen consecutive hours;
then as we flew low over Vancouver, it was setting in a
glory of fire. Somehow, I took the wrong plane out of
Vancouver and landed in Seattle, where I had to wait
for three hours to join the next plane.

It was ten P. M. on October 7, 1961, when finally I
arrived in San Francisco, after a journey which had tak-
en thirty-nine hours in all.

I could hardly believe it when Yvonne ran into my
arms, and for a long time we clasped each other, sobbing together as we cried, "Yvonne, bambina mia," and,
"Mamma, mammina mia."

For three months we stayed in San Francisco; then
we went to the town where Yvonne had lived with
Andy. She got a job as a nurses' aid in a hospital, while
I cared for Rose Anna, my little granddaughter. We had
a small apartment, and we settled down together very
happily. Yvonne did not want to return to Italy; she
liked this country; and if I would stay with her, she
would be perfectly happy.

For myself, I had very little choice. For one thing, I
did not have the money to pay the return fare; I felt
Yvonne and Rose Anna needed me, and besides there
was very little to draw me back to Italy. Romano and

Ernst were not there; the girls were scattered They had their own families and did not need me now, so for the time being I was willing to settle down

I loved the freedom of America. There was so much to interest me, and even at my age, there was much I wanted to learn. Yvonne had an old car which had belonged to Andy, and she had learned to drive; so when she was not working on weekends, we would drive into the mountains or to a lake. I thought the state parks and picnic areas were wonderful, and there were so many breathtaking places to visit, which cost nothing beyond the price of the gasoline. I will never forget my first view of Yosemite, with its mighty rocks and chasms; nor the awe-inspiring redwoods, with trees which had already been growing for thousands of years before Jesus Christ was born.

Life with Yvonne and Rose Anna was quiet and peaceful, and I felt happier than I had in all my married life. There were no disagreements. Yvonne was a good mother, and was popular with everyone who knew her. These first months were like a continual vacation for me.

We moved into a group of apartments, where I was given the position of caretaker. I had very little to do, beyond listening to the tenants' complaints and reporting them, and seeing that no damage was done.

This meant that we had a rent-free apartment, I was earning a small wage, and we were not so isolated.

I was amazed at the opportunities for study which were provided for Americans, whatever age one might be. There were many Mexicans in our community, and I felt I would like to talk with them in their own language, perhaps be able to help them; so I enrolled in a Spanish class. Most of the other students were under twenty; but before the end of the school year, I was on a level with them. Knowing four other languages, especially Italian, made Spanish very easy for me.

I ought to have been perfectly happy, but I always had the sense that something was missing; some part of me had never been satisfied. I volunteered to help in social work, but still there was unrest within me. At first I thought it was because I had not enough to do. After the years of struggle, with never a moment to myself, I believed it was only a reaction. Now I could read without wondering if Giovanni would catch me at it and beat me, and I took out a library card and read voraciously. I joined an artists' group, because I had always had a desire to paint, and enjoyed trying to convey my love of beauty to paper. Yet always at the back of my mind was the sense that my life was still not complete.

Sometimes when I passed a Roman Catholic church, I slipped in, longing in my heart for the faith I had had long ago as a child. I prayed that God, if He heard me, would help me to find once more the belief in Him, which I had lost during the terrible war years, but I came out as empty as I went in.

I worshiped the Creator, for all the magnificence of His creation, but I had no sense of personal involvement; yet as I grew older, I longed for it.

One day a new family moved into one of the apartments. Rose Anna, now almost four years old, asked one of the children if she would play with her. A few days later, Wendy's mother invited me to accompany them to church the next day. Rose Anna could go to Sunday school with Wendy, and I could go to adult church with them; and I gladly accepted.

Yvonne was working at the hospital all day, so Rose Anna, wildly excited, set off with Wendy in her parents' car.

That church service was a revelation to me. The building was without adornment; in fact it was almost barnlike, but there was a sense of joy and expectancy among the people that I had never sensed before. The singing was only mediorce, and the sermon simple and straightforward, but it reached right into my empty heart. Here was something I could understand; there was no condemnation of other religions or denominations, such as I had often heard from the priest.

I had heard so often about God's wrath, the eternal fires of hell awaiting sinners who did not obey what the

holy church ordained; but the simple love of God and
His offer of salvation and forgiveness through the sacri-
fice of Jesus Christ when He died on the cross, had never reached my understanding.

That morning, it was as if I could hear Dr. Margaret's
voice speaking to me. This is what she had tried to tell
me all those many years ago, but I had been too en-
grossed in my own affairs to listen. Now I bowed my
head and cried, "Oh, God, forgive me. I have doubted
You so long; yet You are still willing to forgive. Lord, I
believe You died for me, please cleanse me from my
sin."

A great sense of peace filled me, such as I had never
known before. At the end of the service, the pastor
asked any who wished to accept Christ as Saviour to
come forward; I found myself walking down the aisle,
almost as if some force outside myself had lifted me
from my seat.

Never in all my life had I experienced the sense of
love which poured from the members of that church, as
one after another shook hands with me, and welcomed
me among them.

As I entered our apartment with Rose Anna chattering about what she had done with Wendy, I felt that at
last I had found what I had been seeking for so long.
God was real to me at last; I would never be alone
again. As I thought about it quietly when Rose Anna
was having her nap, I believed that what had happened
was the answer to those prayers of Dr. Margaret long
ago in Switzerland. I longed to tell her that at last I had
found her Saviour, but it was too late, for she had died
many years before; but perhaps even now she knew
what had happened and was rejoicing with the angels in
heaven over the repentance of this stubborn sinner.

I thought of all the years I had gone my own way,
struggling against God's offer of salvation, and I was
humbled before Him. I believed that God had had to
bring me to America to bring me face to face with my
need of Him. Here, I was free from the trappings of the
Catholic church, free from the troubling cares I had en-

dured so long, free even from the business of the work I
had felt was so important  I had been so filled with a
sense of emptiness that at last I was able to realize that
it was only a knowledge of Jesus Christ as my personal
Saviour that could satisfy me. Without Christ, all of the
bad things I suffered and all the good things I did, were
meaningless.

I had need of this new faith in the days that followed,
for a fresh test was before me. Yvonne, Rose Anna, and
I made such a cozy little unit, that I was dismayed when
Yvonne came home accompanied by a man much older
than herself. I took an instant dislike to him, but she informed me that she and Steve were getting married
shortly.

I begged her to think it over; because as far as I could
gather, she knew very little about him. But she replied
that he could certainly be no worse than Andy, and
Rose Anna needed a father. Nothing I could say could
move her. This man was comparatively wealthy and
could provide Rose Anna and herself with a good home
and a life of luxury.

A week later, they were married; and very sorrowful-
ly I had to let them go, although I knew in my heart that
Yvonne was making a terrible mistake.

Now I had to face being alone. I still had the apartment, but did I want to go on living here when Yvonne
and Rose Anna had left. Or should I think of returning
to Italy, if I could somehow save enough money?

I prayed about it, but for the time being, I felt it was
right for me to stay where I was. I had no home to return to in Italy, and I would not go to live with any of
my family. I had just found new friends and a church
where I was welcome, and I believed in my heart that
Yvonne would need me before long. I was sure that this
marriage would never last; and in America people did
not hold the sanctity of marriage, as we had been forced
to do in Italy. Divorce was an easy way out of it.

Why was it, I wondered, that Yvonne, who was so attractive and so loveable, made such poor choices? Then
I remembered what a mistake I had made when I mar-

ried her father. I had not loved him passionately, but I had had no idea of the real man underneath his facade of desire. With the eyes of maturity, I probably judged this husband of Yvonne's in quite a different way from what she did. Experience is a very hard teacher.

So I made up my mind to settle down. Members of the church invited me to their homes; I became involved in various church activities; and I found myself with more true friends than I had ever had before.

It was only two months after Yvonne's marriage, when I fell down the stairs one morning and broke my leg. I was taken to the hospital and was put in plaster; and I knew that I would have to move out of my apartment, for I could not manage the many stairs. I was drawing social security, so I had a little money coming in each week. I had few possessions, because the apartment was already furnished; but where could I find another home?

It was a middle-aged lady from the church, Mrs. Ruth Hemmings, who solved my problem. She visited me in the hospital, then insisted that I go back to her own home until I was able to move about more easily, so on crutches with a full-length plaster cast, I hobbled into Ruth's home, and experienced a loving-kindness such as I had never known previously.

As each day passed, I realized ever more clearly how these people lived out their faith. They loved God, they knew Jesus Christ as Saviour, and their every action demonstrated this love. They lived their faith, instead of talking about it continually. Instead of the fear, reverence, and unquestioning obedience to the Pope and the priests that so many of the poorer people in Italy had known, these people had no fear, only an outgoing joyous sense of love, and a desire to do all things pleasing to God.

It was Ruth who solved the problem of where I should live, by announcing one day that a small Spanish-style bungalow just two blocks away was becoming vacant. She would take me to see it that afternoon. I managed to get in the car, and at the first glimpse of that little house, I knew I could be happy there.

It was small, but had a garden with magnolia and pine trees growing in it. I could hardly believe that it could possibly be my future home.

"But I cannot afford to live in such a place," I faltered.

"It belongs to my husband," Ruth said unexpectedly, "and we want you to have it at a rent you can afford. You must give up the apartment, and we will fix this up for you as soon as it is empty."

I could scarcely speak as I made the short journey back. Never had I met with such kindness. A lump was in my throat, and if I had tried to express my thanks, I would have broken down and wept.

Two weeks later, I moved into my lovely little house. I found that women from the church had gone in and cleaned it for me, and among them, had supplied the necessary furniture. Nothing was new, but it was all clean, and perfectly comfortable; and my cup of thankfulness truly ran over.

I learned that Ruth and her husband owned many such houses. Years ago they had been left a substantial sum of money; and because they had been concerned for many elderly women who were left alone with very little to live on, they had bought houses nearby, as they came on the market; then allowed people in need to use them. This was one of their forms of service for the Lord, and one which gave them great joy.

I heard from Yvonne occasionally, but I knew she was not really happy, though she had a beautiful home, a car of her own, and was continually traveling with her husband. Six months after her remarriage, they were involved in an automobile accident, and her husband was killed. Rose Anna, who had been asleep in the back was only slightly hurt, but Yvonne was severely injured, and had to spend many weeks in the hospital. I had Rose Anna with me again, and how I enjoyed it.

Yvonne came home eventually, a pale, listless creature, but more lovely than ever. She had little to say, and I waited on her patiently until her body and mind had recovered. I had imagined that Steve would have left her well-provided for, but beyond a few, small insurance benefits, there was nothing. The cars, house, business premises—everything—had been mortgaged to the hilt, and there were many debts to pay; so Yvonne came back with nothing more than a bigger collection of unhappy memories.

She seemed to have lost interest in everything; and I often wept in secret for the happy, carefree girl we had loved so much in the years before she came to America.

How patient the friends from my church were with her. They invited her to their homes, on trips to the ocean, to the mountains, and did not take offense when she refused.

Gradually, their repeated kindnesses affected her, and I noticed that she began to take an interest in the various ones who visited her. She never refused to allow Rose Anna to go to Sunday school; but when I had asked her to come to church herself, she had simply shrugged her shoulders, saying that was only for old women; she was finished with all that. I prayed, and I know that many others prayed continually for her also, and I believed that one day Yvonne would awaken to her need.

I was mildly surprised, however, when one Sunday morning she appeared, ready for church, just as Rose Anna and I were waiting for Ruth Hemmings to pick us up in her car.

I must have shown my surprise, for Yvonne laughed shamefacedly, saying, "I thought you and Ruth would be pleased, and it can't do me any harm."

I put my arm through hers, saying, "Honey, this means more to me than you will ever know."

Yvonne looked so sweet and fragile as we walked into church, that I felt inordinately proud, then chided myself for being a conceited old woman; but it meant so much to have one of my children with me at last. Yvonne had very little to say concerning the service, and I was wise enough not to press her; but I know she was touched with the loving welcome given her, and the invitations to join some of the activities.

For three Sundays she accompanied me, with no comment afterward, then on the fourth Sunday, a missionary couple were speaking, and I could see that Yvonne was fascinated by the simple way in which they told of the needs of people among whom they worked. She said nothing until Rose Anna had gone for her nap after lunch; then suddenly, with tears in her eyes, she said, "Mamma, I have given my life to Jesus Christ. I have watched you all these weeks, and Ruth and the other friends who have been so kind to me, and I know that they have a faith which really counts. I've made such a mess of my life so far, but now I want God to take control and make something worthwhile of what is left."

The change in Yvonne from that moment was almost miraculous. Her eyes shone, and how often I smiled as I heard her singing around the house. It seemed that I had been given back my happy, sweet-natured daughter, but she was even sweeter than before.

She decided to go on with nurses' training, and started in a nearby hospital; but she was able to live at home, and what a happy home it was. I was filled with contentment and gratitude to God.

Looking at Yvonne's glowing face, I wondered how long I would keep her; but I prayed that next time there would be no mistake. Several young men made it obvious that they were attracted to her, but Yvonne brushed them off in no uncertain fashion.

Then Ruth Hemmings' son returned from Nigeria, where he was working as a business man, but in a missionary capacity also. From the first moment of meeting, it was obvious that Yvonne attracted him; and as I watched her dreamy faraway expression in the days that followed, I believed that here was the man who would give her the happiness I longed for her. I watched the fragile blooming of their love with almost bated breath, afraid that something might come between them; and Ruth and I often prayed together concerning them.

How delighted we were when they came home together one evening, and with a face of wondering happiness, Yvonne held out her hand to show me the engagement ring on her finger.

"Mark wants to marry me, Mamma," she said, and I held out my arms to them both.

"Will you have me for a son-in-law, Mamma Müller?" Mark asked.

"So very, very gladly," I replied. "I know God will bless you both in the years to come."

"And you won't mind that Yvonne and Rose Anna will go so far away?" he continued.

"I will be proud to think she can share your work, Mark."

Yvonne and Mark were married in the church we had grown to love so dearly. How good everyone was to them, and how gladly I heard Mark and Yvonne exchange their vows so solemnly. This time I knew there was no mistake. Mark would make a wonderful husband and father, and my heart was at rest concerning them.

When at length they departed for their new life, my little house was very quiet, but never lonely. I had so many friends, and God was always with me.

Only a month after Yvonne left, I had a severe heart attack, and I knew that never again would I be as busy and active as I liked to be. I knew, too, that I would never again see Italy or my beloved Switzerland. The journey would be too much for me, and I was content to end my days in this safe, quiet harbor.

I wrote to my family, and heard regularly from them, but I did not mention the heart attack. There was no need for them to worry about me, because I was happier now than I had been for many many years. The burden and struggle of life was over; I had no fear of death, and I felt wrapped around with peace.

It was after this heart attack, when I was forced by doctor's orders to rest and take life very quietly, that I conceived the idea of my story being written down. Maybe after I died, I would leave it for my family to read; there were lessons in it that I myself had been so slow to learn.

This caused me to go back in memory and recall those early days after I lost my parents; and once I began, I could not stop. There were times of joy, times of great exaltation of spirit, but there were many painful memories also.

As I finish now, I am very tired; but there is a great thankfulness in my heart. Like a storm-tossed ship, I have reached a safe harbor, and I can rest assured that the dangers and tempests are over. Through it all, with the mature eyes of faith, I can feel God's leading. How often I rejected Him, yet in His loving compassion He continued to draw me to Him; and I can only say from the bottom of my heart, "My God, how great is thy love and thy mercy to me; while I live my lips shall praise thee."

## More SIGNET Books You'll Enjoy Reading

☐ **THE UNBAITED TRAP by Catherine Cookson.** An unforgettable novel of a young widow torn between the love of a distinguished lawyer and his rebellious, irresistible grown son. (#W6146—$1.50)

☐ **HANNAH MASSEY by Catherine Cookson.** She was caught in a passion-filled conflict between the man she desired and the mother he would destroy. For one of the most magnificently romantic storytellers of today, an unforgettably gripping novel that plunges into the pulsing heart of a family divided by overpowering love, driving ambition and shameful secrets. (#Y6054—$1.25)

☐ **THE FOUNDER OF THE HOUSE by Naomi Jacob.** The first volume of a superb new series, this is the story of the distinguished Gollantz family through the generations—set against an international background full of romance, intrigue, passion and betrayal.
(#Y5622—$1.25)

☐ **THE TALL LADDER by Katherine Newlin Burt.** A beautiful young heiress takes flight to a dangerous western wilderness and meets her match. (#Q6298—95¢)

☐ **THE POELLENBERG INHERITANCE by Evelyn Anthony.** The spellbinding story of a beautiful young woman's search for her father, his clouded past and a mysterious inheritance. "The build-up is inexorable . . . action, romance, international spy stuff, high-level doublecross . . . all expertly welded into a tightly constructed, enormously readable novel."—New York Times Book Review
(#Y5420—$1.25)